Dead Man's Trail

Bev Pettersen

Published by Westerhall Books, 2024.

For the intrepid Liverpool biking gang: Cathy McDonald, Jackie Whynott, Lauren Tutty, Suanne Shankel and Vicki Dyer

CHAPTER ONE

Ricky Lopez spotted the rut in the road seconds too late. His front tire caught in the toothed crack, jerking him to a stop. He flew over the handlebars, the bike cartwheeling above his head. When he hit the pavement, the crack of his helmet filled his ears.

Stunned, he stared up at the blue sky, still gripping the handles, too winded to even swear. Tears pricked his eyes but he blinked them back. Crying was for sissies. And he'd taken worse falls than this. He knew he'd been going too fast, afraid he'd lose his nerve. He just needed a moment to catch his breath, and his courage.

It wasn't a comfortable position. Rocks poked though his t-shirt and the California sun had left the blacktop hot and sticky. Lying on his back feeling sorry for himself wouldn't help either.

"Dammit," he finally managed, his breath still ragged as he sat up and eyed his bike. Remarkably, the front tire looked fine, the worn rubber still plump with air.

He rose to his feet and slapped the dirt off his jeans. Then straightened the bike and gave it an experimental push. Both tires felt okay. The frame had a few more scrapes and the seat was torn but it wasn't damaged enough to stop him. That old bike was damn tough.

His helmet was another matter. The safety buckle had snapped and a new dent pressed into the back of his head. At least it was wearable. He didn't want to give the cops any more excuse to hassle him. His mother freaked out whenever she saw a uniform. She didn't appreciate calls from the truancy officer either, and he felt a stab of guilt that another one was surely on its way. But collecting his pay was more important than a boring day of school.

He rolled the bike forward, pressing down and checking that it really was okay, then swung his leg over the seat and continued pedaling. He had to keep going. Pope wouldn't like him showing up at his home but the man owed him. And cleaning porta potties wasn't anyone's idea of fun, even worse for him if he'd been cheated into working for free.

It was Cedro, his mother's boyfriend, who'd found him the stupid job. Work after school. Cash every Friday. Don't talk about it. A good fit for an enterprising kid who knew how to keep his mouth shut. And Ricky had worked his ass off, setting up portables at concerts and sports events, replacing hand sanitizer and scrubbing cruddy seats.

He'd done it without much supervision too. Pope usually stayed in the truck, talking on his phone until Ricky finished cleaning. Then Ricky was allowed to take a break in the air-conditioned cab while Pope replenished the paper.

It hadn't taken him long to realize that Pope had something else going on. Sometimes Ricky closed his eyes, pretending he was asleep, so he could listen to his boss's curt phone calls. It seemed Pope had several people working for him, and they all needed to know the location of the toilets, as well as the exact time they'd been serviced.

Cedro had warned Ricky not to ask questions. Truthfully, Ricky didn't want to talk to Pope any more than was necessary. He was half scared of the man, although he knew not to show it. People took advantage of fear. And Pope could be erratic.

When he was in a mood, he was downright vicious. Other days he joked and smiled, bragging about all the money he was making. Twice he'd even passed Ricky a hundred-dollar bill, slapping him on the back and calling it a secrecy bonus.

But that had been months ago, back when Pope was still quite normal. Now he was like a junkyard dog, barely civil, even with the guards who controlled the venue gates. Last week he'd tossed a random man against his tailgate, simply for stepping too close to the truck.

And there was that time Pope had driven to a woman's house and she'd yelled and slapped him in the face. Ricky didn't know the reason she was so angry, but he'd been relieved—and surprised—that Pope hadn't hurt her. The man was too unpredictable to expect gentlemanly behavior.

Ricky swerved, just in time to avoid another rut, his thoughts filled with Pope. Maybe the man's aggressive behavior had been reported and he'd lost his job with the porta potty company.

Being fired would explain why Pope had stopped showing up at their regular spot. But that would make it impossible for Ricky to collect his earnings. He didn't know the name of Pope's boss and the magnetic signs on the toilets were regularly changed. Some portables never even showed a company name. Ricky had only asked their employer's name once, and Pope's menacing stare had left him chilled. He'd never asked another question.

It was also possible that Pope had replaced him with a worker who'd finished school, a cleaner who could work full days. But that didn't make sense as Pope never started his route until mid-afternoon. And he'd been satisfied with Ricky, or he'd seemed to be. With Pope, it was hard to tell.

Ricky swallowed and kept pedaling, trying not to dwell on his boss's temper. Cedro said it was best to forget the money. That he'd collect it for him when the time was right. But Ricky wasn't going to sit back and let someone do his dirty work. That would be a cowardly move. Besides, Pope owed him and once you let someone take advantage, there'd be a lineup of people waiting to do the same thing.

No, he intended to collect what was rightfully earned. Or at least try. He wouldn't be stupid about it though. In fact, he wouldn't step too far from his bike, not until he could judge Pope's mood.

He reached down, comforted to feel the outline of the paper stuffed in his pocket showing the total of his hours. That didn't include all the time wasted standing at the pickup spot. Even though Pope had provided him with a phone, the man never bothered to send a text and cancel.

But Ricky didn't plan on mentioning those days. That would be pushing it. Truthfully he'd be happy to pocket half the money he was owed and never see Pope again.

He leaned forward, pedaling faster, letting his grievances feed his energy. The blacktop curved and on the next straightaway he spotted a lone mailbox, rusted and tilted to the side. Barely slowing, he cut onto the rutted driveway.

He'd only been to Pope's house twice but the San Gabriel Mountains were a familiar backdrop. He and his friends spent a lot of time exploring the wilderness park, riding bikes and playing paintball. Or at least they used to. Now his afternoons and weekends were consumed with cleaning toilets.

Even his mother, who was delighted he'd landed a job, had suggested Ricky cut back on his hours. She didn't understand that with Pope it was all or nothing. The man expected people to jump when he spoke. And Ricky had jumped. It was Pope who'd ghosted him. But that didn't mean he'd let the man cheat him out of ninety-two and a half hours of pay.

His fingers fisted around the handlebars, his heart pumping with adrenaline, the same feeling he had before riding down a steep mountain. But this was different than racing his friends. Scarier. And the closer he came to Pope's house, the more his palms stuck to the rubber handles.

He scanned the trees along the driveway. He'd learned to have an escape route when evading park rangers, and it seemed like a smart thing to do now. There were plenty of well-spaced trees on his left, ones that a bike could whip around. Hopefully he wouldn't have to resort to anything so drastic. There was also the chance Pope might feel guilty enough to toss him some extra cash. Of course, that was the best-case scenario.

Just before the driveway straightened, a faded sign said: Beware Of Dog. But Ricky knew there was no actual dog. Pope didn't like them, no matter how many tricks they knew. A dislike of dogs was probably the only thing he and Pope had in common.

Ricky coasted around the bend, skidding to a stop twenty feet from the white stucco bungalow. Pope's powerful truck was parked close to the door. Clearly the man was home.

Ricky studied the house, taking a moment to consider what to say. He hadn't planned much ahead of biking here. It wasn't as though he expected to see Pope relaxing on the porch, drinking coffee and waving a welcome. There was always the possibility the man would refuse to pay up. But Ricky wouldn't be able to look in the mirror if he didn't at least ask.

He checked the yard, hopeful Pope might be outside. But nothing moved except for a bunch of sparrows pecking at the dirt beside a gleaming four wheeler. That machine hadn't been there last month. Pope could afford to buy a brand-new ATV but was too cheap to pay the money he owed. And Ricky's indignation swelled, overriding his fear.

He stepped off his bike. Rolled it to the shaded side of the house and angled it toward a stand of sheltering trees, too narrow for any four wheeler. He hadn't ridden out here to run away. But he didn't intend to be a punching bag either.

Squaring his shoulders, he headed toward the front door. Wide tracks flattened the wizened grass, marking where Pope turned his dually. In one spot, he'd come perilously close to clipping his house. Cedro said a man's driving usually reflected his mood. And Ricky's feet felt a bit heavier.

He knocked twice, quiet and polite. Stepped back and waited. The door didn't open. He gave another series of knocks, this time a bit louder, all the while practicing what he'd say. But the door remained closed.

Pope isn't home. Disappointment warred with relief. He'd ridden his bike a long way, had cut classes to come here. On the other hand, it looked like he wouldn't have to confront Pope, and that man was far more frightening than the toughest school gang.

He turned to go then paused. The truck was here so Pope must be around. This place was too isolated to walk anywhere. Wind rustled through the trees and a hawk screamed overhead, scaring the pecking sparrows. It was so serene he could hear the whirring of grasshoppers. Still, he had a sense of unease, the feeling he wasn't alone.

The front window was open, and he edged along the narrow porch, tilted his head and listened. But no sounds came from behind the fluttering curtain. All Ricky could hear was the pounding of his heart.

It took a moment to realize the noise wasn't from him. It was the sound of snoring. Pope was asleep.

Smiling, Ricky backed away, glad he hadn't knocked too loudly. Pope would be meaner than a badger if disturbed from a deep sleep. But the man would have to get up soon. He generally started his route by mid-afternoon.

Ricky circled to the side of the bungalow, sat down by his bike and pulled out the burner phone Pope had provided. There weren't many minutes left and he should use them up, considering Pope would likely insist it be returned.

There weren't many messages, just a couple of texts from his buddies, warning that the principal was looking for him. Nothing important and no new instructions from Pope. The last one had been four days ago when he'd told Ricky to wait at the pickup spot but Pope hadn't shown. Again.

Seemed like the man had found some other sucker to do his grunt work. The three portables on the truck bed didn't look clean though, so whoever had replaced Ricky wasn't doing a good job. Or maybe these toilets were going in for repair, not to clients.

Ricky rose, walked over to the truck and eyed the portables. They looked like the damaged ones they'd picked up two weeks ago. The signage had been removed but one still had familiar purple graffiti below the side vent.

He swung onto the back of the truck and examined the toilets more closely. Broken handle, damaged door hinge, and missing vent. Definitely the same ones. Which meant Pope hadn't worked in ten days. Weird, but if he hadn't found a replacement worker yet, Ricky might have more leverage to keep his job. And collect his back pay.

He was still fingering the broken handle when a flock of birds flew up from the driveway, scattering over the tree tops. Seconds later, gravel crunched beneath an approaching vehicle. Was someone else sleeping in the house and Pope just arriving home?

Shit. His mouth turned dry remembering how protective Pope was about his truck. And now Ricky was about to be caught standing flat-ass on the truck bed.

CHAPTER TWO

Ricky gulped, dreading the thought of Pope's wrath. He might as well kiss his money goodbye. Already he caught the glint of a brown vehicle through the trees. It was too late to jump down but possibly he could hide. He yanked open the door and slipped into a sweltering porta potty.

There wasn't enough time to completely close the door and sunlight flooded through the two-inch gap. At least he'd be able to see if the driver was Pope.

However, the car stopped close to the house, in front of the truck and out of sight. Then the engine silenced and a vehicle door clicked open. A second door sounded. Seconds later, they both slammed shut.

There was a murmur of voices but neither of the men sounded familiar. Perfect. These visitors could be the ones to wake Pope. Once they were inside, he'd slip off the truck, grab his bike and pretend he'd just showed up. They probably wanted a portable delivered for a last-minute sports function. Pope was always running side deals.

Ricky pushed the door open another inch so he could see the front of the house. Now he could see the backs of the two men. One of them was dressed like Pope, with low-slung jeans and some ink on his neck. The bigger one wore fitted khakis, a polo shirt and walked with authority. Looked like a buyer.

Ricky marginally relaxed. There was less chance Pope would throw a fit with customers around. He just had to wait for a good moment to sneak off the truck.

The men climbed the steps, moving purposefully. The wiry man in jeans gave a sudden hop, pulled back his leg and kicked. Crack! The sound of splintering wood covered Ricky's surprised gasp. He pressed a hand over his mouth and pressed deeper into the portable.

There was a second and third crack. Then the sound of a door caving.

Ricky realized he'd stopped breathing and sucked in a painful gulp of air. He reached out to yank the porta potty door shut then was hit with indecision. The door had been ajar when they drove past. Would they notice if it was suddenly closed?

He didn't know what to do. Cedro called him a quick thinker but now his brain felt like mush. Part of him wanted to latch the door shut. Stay hidden. The other part screamed to grab his bike and hide in the woods.

But the men were talking now, their voices uncomfortably close. As if they were standing by the open window with a clear view of the truck.

Pope's voice was the loudest. "I'm not using. They're lying. I haven't missed any deliveries."

The visitors' voices were calmer, harder to hear.

"Not cutting it either," Pope said. "That's got to be someone down the line."

There was a muddle of voices then Pope spoke again. Speaking faster now. Not quite so loud. "But I'm doing it myself. Keeping it tight, like the boss said."

A sudden thud made Ricky wince. He recognized the sound of fists on flesh.

"Yeah, okay," Pope wheezed, long moments later. "I do have one kid cleaning. Saves me time. But he doesn't know what's going on."

Pope was still talking, claiming he wasn't using. That he hadn't messed with the product. One of the men laughed but it was an ugly sound. Then Ricky heard his name and he jerked back against the toilet seat, his stomach churning.

But they didn't seem to want to listen to Pope and thankfully the voices stopped. Now the only noise was of feet stomping around the bungalow.

He shivered, chilled despite the stuffy heat of the portable but reassured himself that he was safe. The men's beef was with Pope. Once they settled their argument and left, he'd get out of here too. He'd forget the money Pope owed him. Forget he'd ever met the man.

Sweat beaded his forehead while he waited for the men to leave. But now it sounded like they were all back beside the window. Ricky had always heard Pope bossing everyone. Now his voice was different. Subdued, no longer cocky.

"Money is behind the vent, second bedroom," Pope said. "One packet is still on the truck. Uncut, I promise."

Ricky straightened, so horrified he bumped the thin wall. On the truck?

His gaze scrabbled around the portable. Surely Pope meant the cab of the truck, not the porta potties. There was no room to hide anything here. Just in case, he raised the toilet lid. Nothing. And no other place except for the spare paper holder. This was the type of locking dispenser that Pope looked after.

This one didn't appear locked though. He pried at the back with shaky fingers. Pulled back the lid. Felt the blood draining from his face when he spotted the plastic bag. Looked like a brick of cocaine.

For a horrible moment, he couldn't move. Consumed with terror at the realization he'd picked the worst possible place to hide.

He pulled out the packet, his mind racing. He'd toss the bag onto the truck bed. Then they wouldn't have to open the portable. But Pope would know he hadn't left the drugs in the open. And from the sounds of it, they were concerned about its purity.

"Those were rich kids," one man said. "And your habit brought the heat. Wrecking it for all of us, you greedy fucker."

A thud was followed by a cry of pain.

"Was it just you?" the same voice asked. "Everything will be all right. Just tell us the truth."

"Just me." Pope's voice was raspy. "Wasn't trying to steal, just stretching the supply. You know, make us all a bit more."

"Sure, cut it a bit and it goes further. Did you use the portables yourself?"

"Yes, me and the kid. So there's no problem."

"No problem at all," the man said agreeably.

Ricky sagged, relief turning his knees weak. Everything was going to be okay. He should probably step out now. Pope would reassure them that he wasn't a snitch. He lifted his hand toward the door.

Pop, pop.

Ricky jerked back with a yelp then rammed his fist in his mouth. The sound of gunshots wasn't unfamiliar—he lived in a rough neighborhood—but this was way too close. And he had to accept that Pope wouldn't be able to vouch for him. Unless Pope was shooting at his visitors. There had been two shots, so maybe...

He stood stock still, forcing himself to listen. Not to panic.

"Over there," someone said, and for a terrifying moment he thought they were talking about him. But no one rushed from the house. Only two men were speaking though, and he could picture in color what had taken place inside those walls.

The voices moved away from the window. Turned indistinct. This was his chance to run. To escape while they were still inside.

He pushed the door open, keeping a wary eye on the house. Shit. A man's back was in the doorway, his gloved hands gripping a pair of bare feet. Ricky eased the door back to its original position, his heart pounding so fast he thought it might jump from his chest.

He listened in growing terror as the sounds moved closer.

"Damn heavy for an addict," one of the men complained. The truck bed bounced as Pope's body thumped on the back, scant feet from the porta potty door.

"Grab the rest of the product from the shit house. Toss him in the canyon. Then clean up here and dump the truck."

Ricky's heartbeat thrashed in his ears. When the porta potty door opened, his only chance was to kick the guy in the balls, jump over the side of the truck and run. The trees were fifty feet away, his bike twenty. Maybe the gunman wasn't much of a shot.

He pulled in a deep breath, hoping his legs would work, that he'd be able to pedal. But thinking of his bike seemed to draw it to their attention.

"Hey, look over there. Think it belongs to the kid?" The man's voice lowered. "We better check the house again. Boss wants him gone too."

The men stopped talking. Even their footsteps turned quiet, as if they were trying to sneak. Clumsy assholes. He'd hear them in the woods a mile away. And thinking of them as idiots stoked his courage.

He inched open the door, making sure that they'd both crept inside. Then he jammed the plastic bag in the waistband of his jeans and vaulted over the side of the truck.

An angry face flashed in the window, followed by a shout. By then, he was halfway to his bike. He leaped on, found the pedals. Hit full speed in seconds, pumping furiously, his bike a trusty friend. But the trees seemed a mile away and now both men were hollering.

"I've got him!"

He flinched, anticipating a bullet between his shoulder blades. But a branch snapped two inches to his right. A clean miss. Seconds later he was protected by the solid trees. More shots, more curses, but Ricky was grinning now. He even let out a taunting victory whoop.

He kept pedaling, swerving around trees and bouncing over rocks until their shouts faded in the wind. Now it was just him and his life-saving bike.

Along with a kilo of Pope's stolen drugs.

CHAPTER THREE

Gunner isn't as good as the yellow Lab. Nikki Drake immediately felt disloyal. Of course, her German Shepherd couldn't be expected to find the drug cache. He'd had basic training at the K9 Center but drug sniffing wasn't his specialty. Still, it was deflating. Gunner wasn't used to failure, and she'd put him in this position, rushing him into it without proper prep.

He was watching her now, head tilted, trying to figure out what she wanted. His brown eyes gleamed with intelligence but also with frustration. He kept returning to the horse blanket, sitting by it and wagging his tail, hopeful that she'd be happy with his "find."

"He remembers being rewarded when he found the body in the horse blanket," Justin murmured. "When he's confused he reverts to the equine scent."

The yellow Lab was barking, straining at his handler's leash, trying to push past Gunner to the hidden tin of cocaine. That dog was starting to bug her. But Justin was right. Though Gunner was trying to please he didn't understand what was wanted.

She slipped his ball into the drug drawer then repeated the command. "Find."

With the added crutch of the ball, Gunner was able to ignore the blanket. Seconds later he sat by the drawer, tail thumping the floor in triumph. At least now he felt good about himself, but clearly he wasn't ready to search on his own.

"No dog can do it all," the Lab's handler said, his voice smug. "He's oversized anyway. My advice is to keep him focused on protection."

Nikki swallowed her retort. Gunner did much more than protect. Not only did he keep her safe in her PI job, but he'd proven invaluable at search and rescue. There didn't seem to be any reason why he couldn't be trained to find drugs.

But she was a civilian guest, only permitted to use the K9 Center because of Justin's status as a homicide detective. And she was rather sensitive, especially since Gunner had flunked out of this same facility. Admittedly though, he needed more practice with drugs. Along with desensitization to horses.

She pulled open the drawer. Praised him with a singsong voice and rewarded him with his ball then shot a wistful look at the sealed coke tin. If they had access to their own stash, she and Gunner would be able to practice regularly. Not only was the Center a two-hour drive, the facilities were off limits without Justin, which meant the next visit might be weeks away. His vacation days were too scarce to use on dog training.

The Center hadn't always been this strict. She used to be able to book training time. Gunner had even been an esteemed patient at their vet hospital. However, the new officer in charge had introduced restrictive policies, not hiding his resentment that Gunner had turned into a rising star but now belonged to a private investigator. It didn't seem to matter that they were all working toward the same goal.

She clipped on Gunner's leash hoping that next month Justin could book one of the exterior fields. It would be easier to concentrate without being surrounded by other K9s. Her ears hurt from all the barking and she imagined Justin's did as well. His tolerance for clamor was even lower than hers.

Not that he'd ever show any discomfort. He remained motionless at the back of the room, seemingly unfazed by the Lab's high-pitched barking. Of course, he was experienced with both dogs and horses. Next to her, he was Gunner's favorite human. When Gunner had failed the climbing portion of police training, Justin had recognized his potential and purchased him privately.

He'd given Gunner to Nikki, believing she needed a partner in her investigative business. And while Gunner considered Justin part of his pack, she appreciated how Justin never interfered with his handling. When the three of them were home, Gunner was treated like a beloved family pet. But when he was in his work harness, Justin avoided interaction. And that calm professionalism made things easier.

The other handler probably didn't even realize she and Justin lived together. The officer was still bragging about how Labs made better detection dogs and that Shepherds should stick to the protective side of law enforcement.

"Do you know how many scent receptors this breed has?" the man went on, proudly gesturing at his Lab.

"Yes," Justin said. "And a Shepherd has two hundred and twenty-five million receptors. Slightly more than a Lab."

The officer blinked in surprise. "Well, that's true. I guess Shepherds do have more. But Labs have a better nose for narcotics. My dog is a whiz on the scent wall. And you saw what happened when these two went head-to-head."

He moved closer to Justin, almost pushing Nikki aside in his eagerness. "We were updated on the fentanyl deaths. I assume you're no longer calling in outside consultants. That you're here looking for more competent police teams? K9 units that specialize in drugs?"

"No," Justin said, blunt as always.

Nikki caught the twitch of his lip but didn't share his amusement. In fact, the handler's derogatory reference to consultants stung. Certainly the bulk of her work was insurance fraud and surveillance. However, Gunner was on the approved search and rescue list and had been called in to aid police, with excellent results.

In fact, she'd put Gunner up against any K-9 search team. And she wanted to extend that training to narcotics, now that contaminated drugs had impacted her best friend.

Her grip tightened on Gunner's leash as she pictured the despair on her friend's face. Sonja hadn't even realized her brother was an addict until he'd almost died from an overdose. It had left her shattered. Once he'd finished the detox program, she'd taken him to her isolated ranch, determined to break his dependency. But it hadn't been a happy move, for either of them.

Almost overnight, Sonja had switched from being a free-spirited psychic, with a knack for horse betting, to a dogged prison guard mentality. She never left her property, never left Liam alone. She'd turned into her brother's keeper, even demanding Nikki bring Gunner for regular drug sweeps.

While Sonja's belief in Gunner was encouraging, Nikki knew he couldn't be expected to signal for drugs. But Sonja rarely asked for help, and it hurt seeing her so desperate. So if Gunner could be trained, Nikki intended to do it. She just needed to figure a way to jumpstart the process. Because right now, horses were Gunner's kryptonite.

CHAPTER FOUR

"Thanks for arranging the training time today," Nikki said, as Justin maneuvered his truck out of the parking lot and past a high meshed fence. The K9 Center was an all-inclusive facility including rehab and a place where handlers could board their dogs when on vacation. There were also two outdoor fields full of obstacles and scent challenges.

Only forty feet away, a beagle sniffed enthusiastically around a parked car. Seconds later, the K9 rose on his short legs and began pawing at the trunk.

That was the type of focused work Gunner needed. However, it was difficult without a drug supply. And to be of any use, the sample needed to include a wide variety. According to Sonja, her brother had no inhibitions about what he inhaled, ingested or shot into his veins.

Nikki clicked on her seatbelt, mentally reviewing her street sources. With cash and time, she could gather her own drugs. There was a real danger of having her license yanked if she were busted by a cop. On the other hand, her work carried risk. Staying within legal limits was a challenge for most private investigators.

"I wish Tony still ran this place," she said, her wistful gaze fixed on the triumphant beagle. "Gunner can be trained but it's obvious he needs more work."

"Heard a rumor there'll be some changes." Justin reached into his pocket and tossed a container onto her lap. "In the meantime, this will help. At least it'll keep you on the right side of the law."

Nikki picked up the sealed drug container, staring in disbelief at the official K-9 training sticker and its list of contents. "This is super! I can't believe you swiped it."

"I didn't swipe it." Justin shook his head in mock horror. "It's officially signed out. But the way Sonja is pushing, it's obvious your next move would be to hit the street for drug buys. That container has the product and percentages listed. It's also stamped and sealed so law enforcement shouldn't give you grief."

"It's perfect." Her smile widened as she scanned the label. "It even contains fentanyl which is what almost killed Sonja's brother. But I thought the new lieutenant refused to sign out drugs unless they were for official police use?"

"Correct. But a detective from Gang and Narcotics was in there and agreed to put her name on the sheet."

"What do you have to do in return?"

"Look at a crime scene for her. She's heading a special op with LAPD and County. No big deal."

But it was a big deal, and Nikki shifted uncomfortably in her seat. The homicide rate had skyrocketed and Justin was stretched to the limit. Some nights he never slept. It made her doubly grateful she'd chosen private work rather than join a police force. She was able to choose her cases and free up time, in this instance to help a friend.

She only had to finalize a couple of asset searches and reassure a bitter spouse that his divorce settlement was equitable. After that, she'd take Gunner to the track for some training. Horse exposure would help desensitize, moving his training along quicker than working around the house.

"Thank you," she said, gratefully fingering the container. "I know you'll be extra busy because of this. So I'll look after every meal for the rest of the month."

"That just means you decide what we order in."

"True. But I'll also take out the garbage and do the laundry. And you can choose all the activities we do in our spare time."

"Day or night?"

"Both."

Justin turned silent, as if weighing the pros and cons. Then he reached over and squeezed her hand, a wicked grin softening the angle of his jaw.

"Works for me," he said.

CHAPTER FIVE

Nikki clipped her owner's license on her shirt and eased her car up to the security gate at Santa Anita Park, pleased to see the empty lot. It was a dark day—no scheduled races—and traffic was sparse. Training hours closed at ten, so grooms and exercise riders were finished for the morning. The perfect time to train a dog.

Over the last few days, ever since Justin had snagged her the drug tin, she'd practiced in their yard. When asked to search, Gunner was consistently finding the drug cache without the prop of his treasured ball. Whether he would alert to drugs when he was distracted by horse scent would be a bigger challenge, especially since much of his early search training had involved Sonja's animals.

She pulled to a stop alongside the guardhouse and slid a full coffee tray onto the window ledge.

"Good morning, Jim," she called.

"You're a lifesaver," he said, accepting the tray with a wide grin. He waved her through the gate, barely glancing at Gunner.

The guards had never once searched her car or questioned Gunner's presence. It helped that Justin was a longtime horse owner and well acquainted with the head of security. But the power of coffee and a friendly greeting was something her old mentor had stressed.

She parked in the owners' lot, snagging a prime spot close to the barn where Justin's horses were stabled. From the back of her Subaru, Gunner rose and pressed his nose against the window. He loved visiting the track, and her trust in his behavior around strange men had steadily risen.

He leaped from the car, tail wagging, likely thinking he was here to greet some horse friends and perhaps watch a race from the backside. But this visit wasn't for pleasure. She pulled out her pack and slipped on his work harness.

"No races today, Gunner," she said, guiding him toward the barn area. "It's back to school. For both of us."

Though Gunner hadn't completed his training at the police school, he'd proven invaluable in her business, and life. He was a dual purpose K9: He could track as well as apprehend. Unlike most Labs, he had a sharp temperament and could quickly turn ferocious. Though gentle with women and children, his focus was on protecting Nikki. And his learned suspicion of men had led to a few misunderstandings.

Sonja had helped her understand that Gunner wasn't truly aggressive but simply reacting to Nikki's own suspicions. Since he was so attuned, it was important for her to work doubly hard to control her emotions. She certainly appreciated that Gunner had her back, especially since she was a one-person agency.

Besides, she was just as protective of her dog. It still rankled that he'd been labeled by the K9 Center as aggressive and difficult to train. He was actually very adaptable. He might never match a sniffer dog's single-minded purpose, but he should be capable of alerting to drugs.

Her real fear centered on her own training abilities. She'd taken riding lessons as a child but her family had never owned a pet of any kind. Gunner was her first dog and everything she knew was from Justin, along with countless training videos and sessions at the Center.

Shoving away her misgivings, she hurried toward the shedrow where Justin's trainer kept his runners. As expected, the stable area resembled a ghost town. On non-race days, workers wouldn't drift back until the next feeding so this was a good time to work undisturbed.

It was an enjoyable walk, surrounded by the familiar smell of hay and horses. After fighting traffic for an hour, this place was a tonic, and she was totally relaxed by the time she reached the barn.

Several horses stuck their heads over their stall doors, but they knew it wasn't time for supper and quickly dismissed her presence. All except one, a retired bay gelding named Sugar Daddy.

Sugar had been an accomplished racehorse, with over a million dollars in earnings, but now excelled as a companion, or pony horse. He had a regal bearing, with a perfectly shaped white star on his forehead, and his intelligence and confident manner made him an excellent escort for the younger Thoroughbreds.

He was also Sonja's favorite—she claimed they enjoyed "a meeting of the minds." Nikki privately questioned how Sugar could possibly know how horses were training from the other barns. Was there some sort of communication network or did he just see them galloping in the morning? It was all rather hocus-pocus. But there was no arguing that Sonja was eerily successful at picking race winners.

Nikki sighed. She missed Sonja, and no doubt her friend missed the track. Sonja had confided that she now made more money betting than she did from her psychic business. However, she hadn't visited the track since taking over her brother's care. She no longer asked who was entered to race or how the horses were training. Even her animal rescue had been put on hold.

Sugar didn't seem worried about Sonja's absence. He stretched his head over the stall guard, his attention locked on Gunner. Horse and dog sniffed deeply into each other's nostrils, as if gleaning a wealth of information from the contact. Sonja might have known what they were communicating but Nikki had no clue, other than that they'd become good friends.

She gave them another moment to finish their greeting. Then she patted the horse's neck and told Gunner to sit by the stall. She pulled the ball and drugs from her pack, showed them to Gunner and backed away. Both horse and dog watched intently as she disappeared around the corner of the shedrow.

She shoved the ball and drugs between two bales of straw then hurried back. Gunner rose, quivering with impatience, eager to hunt down his ball. Even Sugar watched with pricked ears, influenced by Gunner's behavior.

"Find." She swept her arm toward the rear of the shedrow.

Gunner shot forward, vanishing around the corner. She followed and found him sitting by the hay bale, tail thumping, signifying a successful find.

Too easy. But she'd expected that. He'd already practiced finding a set scent, and he was a wizard at locating his treasured ball.

The challenge was to teach him to alert when she couldn't show him the specific smell. The tin contained eight common street drugs, including animal tranquilizer, cocaine, meth, heroin and fentanyl. A dog's keen nose was unlike a human's and could break the mixture down to each individual component. Hopefully she could train him for any of those drugs, no matter the combo. Especially since Sonja feared her brother would be happy with any mood-altering substance.

Nikki repeated the exercise, each time rewarding Gunner with a happy voice and some ball play. She even included Sugar in the game, giving him a peppermint after every find since he watched with such interest.

Soon Gunner was consistently alerting to the drug tin without his ball. However, they were working in a quiet area and she was running out of hiding spots. At least he'd proven not to be distracted by the horse scent.

She clipped on his leash, deciding he was ready for a different spot. The track kitchen was only a short walk away. When Gunner was confused, he reverted to the equine smell. Likely there would be horse tack tossed in the back of someone's truck. It would be a good test and, if he were successful, a nice way to end the session. She gave Sugar one last mint—he'd been a polite and enthusiastic audience—and headed down the dirt road, cutting between several rectangular shedrows.

The smell of frying onions grew stronger as they approached the kitchen. A motley assortment of vehicles sat in the cafeteria parking lot including several oversized trucks. No one was outside but clearly there were plenty of distracting scents.

She dropped the leash, leaving Gunner in a stay command and walked around the building, looking for a good hiding spot. One that was not too easy but not impossibly hard either.

A two-inch gap below the food dumpster caught her eye and she slipped the drugs beneath the metal frame. Ideally she'd have a second person hide the tin so Gunner couldn't follow her trail. However, considering the contents, she didn't want to enlist anyone's help, and for now, this was enough of a challenge.

She walked back to Gunner and told him to "find." He charged off, delighted to play the game. He stopped briefly by a truck bed filled with scores of soiled horse blankets then lifted his head and raced around the building. By the time she caught up, he was sitting by the dumpster, tail wagging in triumph.

"Good dog!" She pulled his ball from her pocket, rewarding him with his favorite game. They were both engrossed in their play when the back door slammed, cutting the quiet.

A man and woman had stepped outside, lingering on the stairs at the rear of the kitchen. At first their conversation was low, almost secretive, but soon the woman's voice lifted.

"Where is he? You have to tell me!"

The man shrugged and looked past her, noting Nikki's presence. The woman stepped closer, her attention focused on the man. "Please," she said. "You must know."

"I already told you. Wait it out."

"But he's my son! You have to help." She reached out and grabbed his arm.

The man wheeled, shoving her so forcefully she stumbled back, hitting the railing and almost flipping over the side.

Gunner growled. The ball was still in his mouth but his attention was locked on the aggressive man. Nikki clipped on his leash before he could charge to the woman's defense. He had an innate compulsion to help the weak. For that matter, so did she.

"Is everything okay?" she asked, moving closer to the building. The man was younger than she first thought, wiry and fit, probably in his early thirties. She might have considered him good looking if he didn't wear such a cocky sneer.

"Just talking," he called, his voice lowering when he turned back to the woman. "I don't know where he is. And it's best for Ricky if you don't say anything more, understand?"

It was more of a statement than a question but the woman gave a reluctant nod, and the man descended the stairs and walked away, his stride smooth and unruffled.

"Are you looking for someone?" Nikki asked, peering up at the woman. She wore a white apron marked with grease stains and a black hairnet emphasized her delicate features.

"My son, Ricky," the woman said, her voice choking with emotion.

"He's missing and that guy knows something? And won't tell you?" Nikki stopped at the bottom step and glanced around for a guard. It was tempting to follow the man and question him herself. With Gunner's help, he'd likely turn helpful. But the risk of being banned from the track was too great. Justin knew the head of security, but a dog bite wouldn't be overlooked.

"Cedro keeps insisting he doesn't know where he is." The woman's voice was so low it was almost inaudible. "Maybe he doesn't. All I know is that I haven't seen Ricky in three days. And I don't know who else to ask."

"Have you notified the police?"

"Yes, they said they'll keep a lookout. The truancy officer thinks Ricky is just avoiding school." The woman placed her hands over the railing, as if needing it for support. "He's cut classes before. He does well at school but thinks some of his teachers are useless."

So the police probably aren't looking too hard, Nikki thought. "And what do you think?"

The woman just shook her head, her mouth pinched with worry.

"How old is Ricky?"

"Twelve."

Nikki kept her face impassive but her concern rose. "Where does he usually go when he skips? Does he stay with a friend? Go to a mall?"

"No, they hang out in the wilderness park. But he always comes home to sleep." The woman's voice cracked. "That's why I think the truancy officer is wrong. This time feels different."

Nikki glanced in the direction Cedro had taken, thinking of Sonja and Gunner's training, and the insurance claim she'd been paid to investigate. But she didn't think long. This kid was only twelve.

"Maybe I can help," she said.

CHAPTER SIX

Ricky's mother sat in the passenger seat of Nikki's car, nervously chewing her fingernails. Her name was Andrea Lopez, and she'd gratefully accepted the offer of a drive home. She worked six days a week at the track kitchen and the smell of onions and frying bacon clung to her clothes.

It was only a ten-minute drive to her apartment in Monrovia and once she realized Nikki was a private investigator, she spoke openly about Ricky, as if comforted to have a sympathetic ear. Though she admitted he sometimes skipped school, she insisted he always came home at night. And the fact that she hadn't seen him in three days—and that Cedro was uncharacteristically brushing her off—left her even more worried.

On an optimistic note, she believed Ricky was okay. He'd texted, telling her not worry but wanted to stay away for a while. He hadn't given a reason but his jacket and backpack were missing, along with half a loaf of bread and their big jar of peanut butter.

"I shouldn't have told the cops he took that stuff," Andrea said, with more than a twinge of bitterness. "They're never any help. They think he's using home as a base but that I'm working too much to notice. Said it's more of the truancy officer's concern."

She lowered her hands, wringing them in her lap. "And I pushed him to take that job. He likes to be outside but that's when he started with all the late nights."

"What's the job?" Nikki asked, slowing her car as she drove past a long line of identical-looking apartment buildings.

"Cleaning portables. It was supposed to be only a few hours after school, but most nights I'm in bed by the time he finishes. I work so early that I barely see him. Maybe I am working too much. But I'm a single mom. I have to make money."

"What's the name of the portable company?"

"Don't know." Andrea's voice thickened with guilt. "Ricky never says much. There were so many questions I should have asked. I was just glad he had a job."

"But where did he go to work? Who hired him?"

"Someone called Pope. He drives the service truck and picks Ricky up close to the school."

"Do you know the spot?"

Andrea nodded. "At the intersection close to the Mount Wilson trailhead. It's convenient because the street runs to the school and there's a bike rack. Pope gave Ricky a phone so he could tell him when to meet. Ricky's only supposed to use it for work but sometimes he texts me on it. It doesn't have any location services."

Now they were getting somewhere. "Did the police try tracking it?"

"No. They only had me call him, but his cell must be out of minutes. Or maybe he's in a dead spot in the wilderness park. He's a bit of a daredevil."

"On his bike?"

"Yes, the park rangers have warned me before. He can do amazing things but they worry about his safety. I've seen videos of him stunting. But there's nothing new on his social media, and I've called all his friends. They haven't heard from him either, not since the day he skipped school. He must be all right because he came home to get the food. But it's all very strange." Turning her head, she resumed biting her nails.

Nikki checked her rearview mirror. Gunner was lying in the back, his tongue lolling in a contented smile. He looked pleased to have another passenger in the car, as if anticipating a fun job. And Andrea seemed like someone who needed help.

It was only mid-afternoon. It wouldn't take much time to swing by Ricky's meeting spot. If only to make sure he wasn't lying in a ditch. Hurt or worse.

"Text me a picture of Ricky." She pulled a business card from her console and passed it to Andrea. "Along with a picture of his bike."

Andrea nodded but fingered the card gingerly, as if it were hot to the touch. "How much will this cost? My next payday isn't for another week, and, well, there's never much left."

"No charge," Nikki said cheerfully. "Gunner and I need some exercise. Was it yesterday when you noticed Ricky's pack was gone?"

"No, that all happened two days ago."

Nikki nodded but her chest tightened. The Mount Wilson trail led into the foothills of the San Gabriel Mountains and was a popular gateway to the Angeles National Forest. Its rugged terrain covered over 650,000 acres, with elevations up to 10,000 feet.

"That's my apartment." Andrea leaned forward, gesturing at a run-down building with two numbered doorways. "The one on the left. And the curtains are shut. Ricky's home!"

She grabbed the handle, pushing the door open before the car came to a full stop.

"I don't need your help now." Her words rushed together in excitement as she stepped out. "But please come in. You can tell him how much worry he's caused. He'll listen to someone like you better than me."

She slammed the door shut and hurried toward her apartment, so eager she almost tripped over the curb.

Her relief was contagious. Smiling, Nikki opened the back door and motioned for Gunner to jump out. She'd been raised by a single mom and empathized with the challenges. No doubt, Ricky believed he had good reason to take off, but he needed to understand how hard it was on his mother. At least this disappearance had a quick and happy ending.

CHAPTER SEVEN

Nikki stepped inside the apartment with Gunner at her side. She could hear Andrea rushing down the hall, calling to her son. Moments later, the woman re-appeared, a confused look on her face.

"He's not here," she said. "But he was in his room. Left it in a big mess."

The sitting room and kitchen were also in shambles. Drawers were upended and sofa cushions had been thrown against the wall. The freezer door was open and water dripped on the linoleum floor. Ricky may have disappeared again, but not before vindictively trashing his mother's home.

"Did you have a recent argument?" Nikki asked. "Or maybe he had a fight with someone else in the family?"

"There's no one else." Andrea pivoted, frowning as if only now absorbing the mess. "And he's a good kid. We don't fight. I leave for work before he gets up so there's no time for arguments. Everything was normal. I don't understand why he'd do this."

"Does anyone else have a key?"

"No, but the window is open in his room." Andrea gestured and headed back down the cramped hall.

Nikki followed her into a tiny bedroom at the rear of the apartment. Clearly Ricky loved extreme sports, especially when they involved bikes. Posters were pinned over the walls. In one, a rider was descending a steep cliff on a robust black bike with knobby tires. Another pictured a desert scene with the bike rider brandishing a paintball gun. But the posters were the only things still in place.

The mesh window screen had been kicked in. A student desk was overturned, its drawers pulled out and tossed aside. Paper littered the floor. Even the mattress had been flipped, one end leaning haphazardly against a crooked headboard. A set of headphones had been ripped apart.

Andrea pressed a hand to her mouth, eyes wide with dismay, and embarrassment. "On hot days we need the breeze," she said. "So we leave the window open. But I don't know why he'd tear the screen unless he lost his key. And he saved his money for months to buy those headphones."

"I don't think it was him," Nikki said slowly. This room had been searched. Unsuccessfully, considering the spiteful destruction of the headphones. And how the freezer door had been left open.

She glanced at Gunner who sat politely on his haunches. He kept glancing toward the kitchen, more interested in checking the smells coming from the thawing food.

Nikki scooped up a scatter of papers, noting the high marks. Ricky might habitually cut classes but academically he seemed to be doing well, just as his mother had claimed.

"What would he have?" Nikki asked. "That someone would want?"

"Nothing. He talked about saving money for a new bike but uses most of his earnings for groceries. I doubt there was even forty dollars in here. And he doesn't own many electronics. Uses a school computer for social media. He really doesn't have anything worth stealing."

Nikki nodded. But parents didn't always know what their kids were doing. And Ricky's bedroom had been searched more thoroughly than the rest of the apartment.

"I'm going to drive out to his pick-up spot," she said. "Take a look around. In the meantime, check if anything is missing. And file a police report."

She glanced at his open closet. The wire hangers were empty, all his clothes dumped on the floor. "Give me his favorite shirt. One he wore recently that hasn't been washed."

Andrea pulled a faded T-shirt from the pile of clothing. "He sleeps in this. When he's home to do it."

"Okay," Nikki said. "Be sure to text me his picture. Along with one of the bike."

She wheeled toward the door. A daredevil kid, uncharacteristically missing for three days, and his room tossed. She didn't look back, knowing it best if Andrea didn't see the concern on her face.

CHAPTER EIGHT

Nikki stopped close to the Mount Wilson trailhead and checked her phone app. The satellite map confirmed the road ran to the school and was the spot where Ricky was picked up for his job.

She took several pictures of the bike rack. Five bicycles were locked in place but a comparison to the photo Andrea had sent showed that none were Ricky's. Which might mean he was still on his bike...or lying beneath it.

She followed the side of the road, grimly studying the terrain. It was steep, covered with loose rocks and prickly shrubs, but Gunner would have no problem as long as he was off leash. If Ricky had pushed his bike up the hill, Gunner might be able to pick up his trail. It was definitely not an inviting spot to ride unless one was both skilled and daring.

She returned to her car, tugged on her hiking boots and gathered her pack, making sure the usual contents were enclosed: dog boots, water, collapsible bowl, plastic bags, handgun, pepper spray, knife, fly repellant, survival blanket, first aid kit, Narcan nasal spray, zip ties, binoculars, protein bars, and dog kibble. Gunner gave an excited whine, knowing what the pack meant. She clipped on his work harness, let him sniff Ricky's shirt and gave the "find" command.

Gunner scrambled up the side of the canyon, nose to the ground, slanting left then right. She followed more gingerly, picking her way along an erosion cut, skirting poison oak and prickly balls of sage. Heat rose from the ground and a lizard sunned itself on a rock, loath to move. Already, sweat trickled down the back of her neck and her shirt stuck to her skin.

Gunner searched enthusiastically, handling the conditions with ease. A startled rabbit burst from the chaparral and he paused, front leg cocked then resumed casting for the target scent. She watched with a sense of pride, remembering the long hours they'd practiced at Sonja's property. He may never make a dependable drug sniffer but he was a tremendous tracker.

However, the ground was dry and scenting conditions were challenging. There were also other unofficial entry points, especially for adventuresome kids. Gunner cast around for another fifteen minutes but it was obvious there was nothing to find. Sometimes no sign was good news. In this case though, Nikki wasn't sure.

She called him back, poured some water in his bowl and phoned Ricky's mom.

"No sign of him here," she said.

"I'm glad you didn't find him," Andrea said. "That he didn't crash his bike and was lying on the ground all alone."

Nikki rubbed her hot forehead, sharing the woman's relief, but not totally comforted. "Could he have entered at another spot? Maybe the official trailhead?"

"No, the kids never go that way. They want to stay after the park is closed."

"It's steep here. Do they always take their bikes?" It would be easier for Gunner to pick up the trail if Ricky was on foot. A bike was a tough ask.

"The steeper the better. He's always coming home with cuts and bruises." Andrea's voice turned defensive which it seemed to do whenever she believed her parenting skills were being questioned. "I've warned him but he doesn't listen. All his friends do the same thing."

"And none of them have heard from Ricky? They have no idea why he took off?"

"No, I called them all. And everything was normal at school. One of his friends said Ricky hadn't been paid lately. But I didn't know about that."

"Maybe it was something with his job that's bothering him." Nikki walked over to a nearby portable and snapped a picture of the name and number posted on the side. It shouldn't be hard to find out where he worked. She just had to check all the portables within a certain radius. Then call the companies.

"I'll see who owns the porta potties," she added. "Find his employer that way."

"But he didn't work in that area," Andrea said, dashing Nikki's plan. "His boss picked him up there because it was close to the school, and his bike could be locked in the rack. Then they drove places."

"Places?" Nikki had to work hard to hide her frustration. Pulling information from Andrea was slow work.

"School and sports events, concerts, places like that. It was Cedro who found him the job. But he doesn't know the company either."

"What about Pope's full name? Cedro must know it."

"He says he doesn't. That it was just a job posting in the track kitchen." But Andrea's voice was troubled as if she wasn't so certain.

Nikki wished she'd questioned Cedro earlier, before he had the chance to walk away. She couldn't imagine not wanting to help, unless he was involved. "What trainer does Cedro work for? Does he live at the track? And what's *his* full name?"

"Cedro Rugger. He has a dorm room but he doesn't work around the horses. He's with maintenance. Maybe he'll be in a better mood tomorrow. He drops by the kitchen every morning for his break. I'll ask him again."

Nikki didn't intend to wait for Cedro's mood to improve. She'd find him on her own. Today. And if he worked with maintenance, that meant he was employed by the track which would make information easier to obtain. The track kept better records than most trainers. But there was an odd change in Andrea's voice, a softening when she spoke about Cedro.

"What's your relationship with him?" Nikki asked.

"We used to date. Not anymore."

"Maybe he has a temper. Did you not want him around Ricky?"

"No! He and Ricky get along great. He was good to us."

Nikki felt her mouth tighten. She'd seen the way Cedro had shoved Andrea. Gunner had picked up on the aggression as well. Andrea was so quick to turn defensive. It made her opinions—and allegiances—somewhat dubious.

Nikki changed her line of questioning, knowing it wouldn't help to antagonize Ricky's mother. The woman might turn even less helpful. "Did you file that police report on the break-in?"

"Yes," Andrea said. "But nothing was stolen so the police aren't sending anyone by. They told me to keep the windows locked."

"Good idea," Nikki said, concerned by the mess left in Ricky's room. Maybe it was smart for him to stay away, to hide out somewhere. Clearly he'd made someone angry. And whoever was looking for him certainly knew his address.

CHAPTER NINE

Nikki drove back to the racetrack and began her search for Cedro, starting at the track kitchen. When she'd seen him earlier, he'd veered to the right, cutting behind a shedrow, as if heading to work. It was feeding time so there'd be plenty of grooms around. Likely someone would know him.

Gunner glanced toward Justin's barn, as if wondering why they were walking in the opposite direction. She gave his head a reassuring pat. "Just taking a walk, boy."

With no scheduled races, the backside was relaxed. Smiling grooms joked and chattered as they fed their charges the last meal of the day, and horses pulled contentedly at their haynets. Colorful flowerbeds connected neighboring barns, and she waved at several familiar faces.

It was actually a treat to walk around and not be focused on dog training or an upcoming race. It gave her time to appreciate the flexibility of her job and simply drink in the surroundings. The scenery was stunning, with horses, graceful palm trees and the San Gabriel Mountains towering in the background.

There was also lots of space: over three hundred acres with sixty-one barns, or shedrows, as well as office trailers and worker dorms. The closest maintenance building was near the washroom facilities by the dorms. That coincided with the direction Cedro had been heading.

She asked several workers if they'd seen Cedro Rugger. None of them knew him except for a young woman who was hosing a horse's leg.

"This time of day," the groom said, "he's probably closing the maintenance building." The woman's expression remained blank, making it hard to gauge her opinion of Cedro.

Nikki thanked her and headed toward the maintenance building. Almost immediately she spotted a man locking the door of a cinder block building, his back to her. He closed the padlock with a clink and turned around. Bingo.

Cedro stared for a moment then shook his head. "I told Andrea I don't know where her kid is," he said. "So if you're here about that, keep walking. Otherwise, I'm always happy when a beautiful lady wants to follow me home."

"I just want to know where Ricky works," she said, suppressing an eye roll. Cedro had an inflated opinion of his appeal to women.

"What's it to you?" He jangled his key ring, his gaze lowering to the horse owner's license clipped to her shirt. "Rich people like you don't care about kitchen workers. Besides, I don't know where the kid worked."

"Yet you found him the job."

"Is that what Andrea said? I don't remember it like that. Now I'd love to chat but I have a job to do." He gave a suggestive wink. "Unless there's something else you'd like me to help you with?"

"Does your job include working with porta potties? Now that Ricky is missing?"

Something dark flashed across his face. "I oversee sanitation," he snapped, all hint of flirtatiousness gone. "Nothing to do with portables. And Ricky is none of your damn business."

"He certainly is." Nikki flipped open her PI license, noting the surprise on Cedro's face, and possibly a hint of alarm. "I need the name of his boss," she went on. "Or the company. That's all. I just want to bring him home."

"Don't have a name," Cedro said. "I just told Ricky about a posting on the notice board. He must have followed up on his own."

"So you're saying you don't know Pope?"

"Was that his name? Like I keep telling Andrea, I don't know anything more. Guess you'll just have to believe me."

His swagger had returned along with his leer, making her teeth grit. Gunner gave a low growl. He always knew her feelings, no matter how hard she tried to hide them. But it was infuriating that this man would refuse to help a kid, and it didn't take a smart dog to sense he was lying.

"And keep that mutt away from me," Cedro added. "Or I'll kick his damn teeth in."

"That's not how it would go," she said. It was unfortunate they were on track property. Despite his bravado, Cedro kept a wary eye on Gunner and appeared to have a healthy respect for dogs. He also seemed to know that Gunner wasn't bluffing.

"Is Ricky hiding in the mountains?" She took a step closer, pushing for an answer. "Did something happen to him on the job?"

Cedro's body language changed, his shoulders squaring, his eyes sparkling with sly intelligence.

"Speaking of on the job," he said suddenly, loudly. "Quit with the hundred questions. You're harassing me at my workplace. Is your dog even licensed to be here? Wonder what would happen if I reported a dog bite."

Nikki hid her dismay. A bite report, even if it was trumped-up, wouldn't be ignored and it was unfortunate that this man knew it. It negated the Gunner factor.

"Your lack of cooperation makes me think you know Pope," she said, just as loudly. "And probably why Ricky is hiding. So I'm doubly glad I accepted this case. And I'm not stopping until I find him."

"Be careful, PI lady," Cedro said. And somehow his lowered voice was even more threatening. "Your fancy licenses mean nothing to me. And accidents can happen around the barns. So you better worry about your own horses' health instead of some kid you never met."

"I will find him," Nikki said, holding his flat stare. "With or without your help. And if I learn you had knowledge you refused to share, you'll be hearing more from me. As well as the authorities."

"Oh, no, the *authorities*," Cedro mocked. He didn't seem at all worried and even had the gall to respond with a promise of his own: turning his key ring and pointing it at her, in the shape of a gun.

CHAPTER TEN

"You wouldn't believe that Cedro guy," Nikki said, later that night as she rehashed events to Justin. "He even threatened our horses."

Justin chuckled, shifting on the bed and adjusting her head on his shoulder. "He must be an idiot to threaten a tough PI like you. Next time, take Gunner."

"I did have Gunner."

"Then he's reckless. Possibly dangerous."

"He's definitely cocky. He might not know where Ricky is, but he has an idea why he ran. I'll talk to the security guards. Find out if they've had any complaints. I need to squeeze him a bit."

"Check with Travis Hillman. That'll save time. And I'll hire a private guard for the horses, as a temporary measure. So you have one less thing to worry about."

Nikki gave his cheek a grateful kiss. Justin never discounted a threat. Cedro might be all bluster but it would be comforting to have someone whose only job was to protect their horses. And she'd met Hillman, head of security, a few times. He'd worked with Justin at the LAPD before accepting the track job. Just last month he'd dropped by their barn to help celebrate a stakes win. Sonja had met Travis as well and pronounced him a genuine horse lover. That had been the last time she'd visited the track.

Sonja had been so carefree back then, gleefully picking winners, making psychic believers of them all. Now she'd chained herself to her brother's side, determined to break his drug dependency.

"How did Gunner's training go?" Justin asked, as if sensing the direction of Nikki's thoughts. "Was he able to ignore the horses?"

"Improving. He found the tin without his ball, but I didn't hide it very well. The horses don't sidetrack him anymore but I'm not sure if he would consistently alert to drugs. He was happier when we went to the wilderness park looking for Ricky."

"Not surprising. He loves a challenge, and trailing is the hardest of the disciplines. It takes a special dog to work off-leash, think independently. You'll still get plenty of police business doing that."

She rolled on her back, not caring if Gunner ever made the drug consult list. She just wanted to help Sonja. Besides, there was always a demand for his talents. The police unit had sufficient tracking teams— the nose to ground K9s that could follow a set of footprints, find cadavers, or sniff out drugs. Typically, those types of dogs worked on a leash.

But trailing dogs required a different skill set. They followed a smell pattern, on the ground or in the air, wherever it led. Sometimes the trail deviated from the actual track, depending on wind and weather conditions, which is why they needed freedom to work.

She and Gunner had worked hard to hone that ability and to learn as a team. Sonja's ranch with its multitude of rescue animals had played a key part in his training. And while it was nice to know the police valued Gunner's trailing skills, Sonja needed his help now. Finding drugs. So that's what Nikki intended to do. Unless there was some reason why he shouldn't.

She peered over at Justin, respecting his opinion. "Do you think Gunner's too old to learn?"

"Hell, no. He's only three. But you both enjoy search and rescue more than anything else. I don't think Sonja understands what she's asking. She can't seriously think she can keep an addict away from drugs if he's set on finding them."

Justin had a way of cutting to the root of the problem. Sonja's request that Gunner sweep her property for drugs was rather extreme. But her brother's overdose had left her reeling, and Nikki empathized with her determination to help. Family was precious.

"I'd probably try the same thing if my sister were still alive," she said. "Besides, it's annoying when your cohorts are so dismissive. Just because Gunner didn't finish K9 training, they think he's only good for guard work."

"That's because his protective instincts are very much in evidence when they step close to you," Justin said dryly. "And there are rumors of his exploits, along with a few bad guys with scars."

"Point taken." She glanced at Gunner who was sprawled on his dog bed. His eyes were closed and he looked so peaceful it was hard to imagine he'd saved her life. More than once.

"I'll talk to Sonja again," she said. "Let her know how much training it involves, and that he might never be consistent. She seems to think he's capable of learning anything. And quickly."

"Well," Justin said, "she's usually right. She does have a gift."

Nikki blinked, scanning his face again. While she'd learned to respect Sonja's psychic abilities, it was way more difficult for a clinical detective like Justin. And though he appreciated Sonja's feedback on his horses, he was a long way from requesting her help with a murder case. Or so Nikki had thought.

"Is that why you've been asking her opinion on the horses? You've been checking her out? Testing her?"

Justin remained impassive, not giving anything away. Then a smile tugged at the corner of his mouth and she could feel laughter rumbling in his chest. "I admit I was curious, especially since some of the horses she nailed were absolute longshots. She claims she has a special affinity with Sugar. Apparently he doesn't know words but transfers in pictures. So she sees when a horse is confident, happy, and feeling competitive. If the favorites don't like their shoes, the ground, the weather, their hay, or simply had a restless night, she'll toss them and go for the overlay."

Nikki sighed, fingering the edge of the sheet. Maybe she was the closed one. She'd not asked Sonja many questions about her psychic gift, admittedly felt uncomfortable. Yet Justin, who she considered more of a skeptic, already understood more about her friend's channel with Sugar.

"So you might ask for her help with police cases? Down the road?"

"I'll use any tools available," Justin said, "if they'll help me nail a killer and give closure to a family."

His successful ending was so much different than hers. Finding someone, bringing them home alive, was her ultimate goal. Tragically, Justin's cases started with a dead body. He probably didn't receive much appreciation either, considering the devastated family would also be facing a long and agonizing murder trial.

For her, a thank you was the best reward of all. It left her walking on air, pumped to begin the next search. She didn't think she'd be able to handle the darkness of Justin's job.

"Thanks for encouraging me to be an investigator." She pressed a grateful hand against his chest. "Helping me get a foothold in search and rescue. My job is so much easier than yours."

"No, it's not, Nik. I worry about you every day. Never knowing what you'll encounter. Working alone, with no backup."

His admission surprised her. He was usually so cool, never interfering with her job or the cases she took. And she needed that from him. His insouciance gave her confidence.

"But I have Gunner," she said lightly. "He's always ready for anything."

"Yes, and he's the only reason I sleep at night."

She laughed. Justin didn't.

CHAPTER ELEVEN

The morning sun burnished the back of the grandstand with a golden hue, filling Nikki with fresh optimism. Someone at the track had to know more about Cedro and his porta potty connection. The owners' parking lot was busier than yesterday but she found a spot close to the gap where the horses entered the track.

It was eight o'clock and the Thoroughbreds were still training, some jogging along the outer rail while others pounded around the oval, tails streaming in a serious workout. Rapt owners watched from Clockers' Corner, joining their trainers over breakfast and coffee. If Justin were here, he'd be able to point out the more established runners, but there were over two thousand horses stabled at Santa Anita and she only recognized the ones from their shedrow.

"Morning, Nikki," a woman called, stopping a gleaming bay horse alongside the rail. "Heading to the barn? Heard you were around yesterday but it must have been after I left."

"Hi, Colleen." Nikki smiled up at the rider mounted on the intelligent-looking bay with the white star on his forehead. Now that was a horse she knew well. She'd probably fed him ten mints yesterday during Gunner's training session.

"How's Sugar this morning?" she asked, stepping closer to the rail. "Keeping the youngsters in line?"

"Definitely." Colleen loosened her reins, giving Sugar a well-deserved break. "We brought over that gray two-year-old. Just waiting for him to finish. This is his first day to go around on his own."

Nikki followed Colleen's worried gaze to a leggy Thoroughbred who was shying at a green trash bin by the grandstand. The colt acted young, spooking at all the sights. It was remarkable that the exercise rider could even stay in the saddle. It emphasized the importance of the track ponies, especially when they were as smart and steady as Sugar.

Unlike Colleen, Sugar paid no attention to the young horse's antics. He stuck his head over the rail, more interested in greeting her than babysitting. He sniffed at her backpack then her pockets, hopeful for a mint.

But Nikki couldn't linger by the rail, not with Gunner. She didn't want to jeopardize his informal track privileges, especially after Cedro's threat. The man knew only licensed service animals were allowed, and how quickly dogs could be banned. Still, Colleen was at the track every day and knew a lot of people. Nikki didn't want to waste this opportunity.

"Do you know Cedro Rugger?" she asked, lowering her voice. "Works in maintenance?"

"Don't know the name, maybe the face." Colleen twisted in the saddle as the loose horse siren abruptly blared. "Shit. The grey just dumped his rider."

She swung Sugar around on his haunches, calling over her shoulder. "Tell Sonja we have three horses entered for the weekend. And that Sugar is ponying them."

Nikki nodded as Colleen galloped away but knew the information would be met with indifference. Sonja used to request an update on every horse Colleen escorted, along with race conditions. Not anymore. Her only concern now was her brother, along with a willingness to go to any extreme to monitor his activities.

Nikki lingered by the rail, watching the unfolding drama. Loose horses were unpredictable and could cause all sorts of trouble. However, Colleen and Sugar quickly reached the frightened gray, which trotted to Sugar's side seconds before a speedy outrider galloped up.

Sugar is definitely special, Nikki thought, joining the horsemen around her in a collective sigh of relief. Relaxing, she turned away and continued toward the kitchen, pressing Sonja's number as she walked.

"Is Gunner ready?" Sonja asked, not even bothering with a greeting. "Hope you're bringing him out today. Liam does repair work in the morning but usually goes for a hike in the afternoon. That gives us a chance to check his room. The barn too. Addicts are sneaky."

She went on about the importance of keeping Liam away from people, where she intended to hide surveillance cameras, and how she didn't dare leave the property, even to buy groceries. It was unsettling to hear her so frazzled. Always before, she'd been the steady voice of wisdom.

"I'll pick up your groceries," Nikki said, once Sonja paused to take a breath. "But Gunner needs more training. This is different from his usual work. And using him seems a bit extreme. Liam's privacy—"

"Liam almost died! And he begged me to help. So I need to be heavy handed. Yes, it's different. But I know Gunner can smell that crap. He just needs to know it's important to you."

Nikki fingered the strap of her pack, tamping down her ping of guilt. Sonja wasn't wrong. The drug tin was in there but beside it was the plastic bag containing Ricky's shirt. She'd been more enthused about finding a missing kid, not on training Gunner for a single task, one that left her ambivalent.

"Besides," Sonja went on, "it might help you too."

"What do you mean?" Nikki straightened. "Do you see something? I thought you were taking a break."

"I'm not doing any paid work. My energy is too depleted. But I can't help seeing things." Sonja's voice broke. "That's why I'm so worried about Liam. There's a darkness around him, probably involves drugs."

Nikki sighed and veered around a groom tossing straw bales from the back of a truck. She'd benefited from Sonja's psychic gift in the past but it wasn't all rainbows and unicorns. Sometimes Sonja saw things she didn't want to know, and sometimes they helped with Nikki's cases. Sometimes, not.

"I know you're concerned about Liam," Nikki said. "And I want to help. But do you sense something else? Something that could help me find a missing boy?"

"No, my energy is too messed up. I only see drugs around both you and Liam."

Not surprising, Nikki thought, considering she had a drug sample stuffed in her backpack and had been handling it for days. And it wasn't fair to be asking for help when Sonja needed unconditional support.

"I'll drop by around three," she said, shoving aside her concerns about Liam's privacy.

"And you'll ask Gunner to check Liam's room?"

"Yes. But Gunner's not consistently alerting to drugs yet, even when I show him the exact scent. And that can't happen at your place since we have no idea what we're looking for."

"Liam doesn't play favorites." Sonja's laugh lacked humor. "Meth, coke, horse tranquilizer, whatever's available. And since it's often cut with contaminants, it's like playing roulette. He's seen friends drop dead on the street. I'm just learning how badly he's addicted and it's terrifying. I even caught him searching my purse for money. At least I have that naloxone kit you dropped off."

"Send me your grocery list," Nikki said, her heart aching for both Sonja and Liam. "I have to stop by the barn first. After that I'll head to your house and see what Gunner can find."

CHAPTER TWELVE

Nikki left Gunner beneath the shade of the same tree as she had yesterday then circled to the front of the cafeteria and stepped inside. Most of the tables were full, and the air was thick with conversation and the mouthwatering smell of bacon.

A dented bulletin board hung by the entrance and she stopped to check the listings. Nothing was posted about cleaning portables, only listings for hot walkers, grooms, and an exercise rider who wasn't afraid of bucking horses.

She turned away and zigzagged around the tables. Gunner couldn't be left alone for long. He wouldn't break his stay command, not unless he thought she needed help, but he also wouldn't roll over if a man approached in a threatening way—or in what Gunner perceived as a threat.

Right now, people at the track viewed him as an imposing but gentle Shepherd, one who was quiet and good with horses. There'd never been any complaints. But it took a long time to build a dog's reputation and only one incident to wreck it. And Cedro's threat of reporting a fictitious dog bite was worrisome.

She scanned the room, searching for Andrea. The cafeteria line was long and heads bobbed as plates of steaming food slid across the counter. But Andrea wasn't visible at the front of the kitchen or behind the cash register.

Nikki squeezed between two tables, peering past a stocky man, and finally spotted the woman at the rear of the kitchen, shaking oil from a basket of fried potatoes. She glanced up, saw Nikki and gestured toward the back door.

Nikki nodded and slipped back outside, collecting Gunner as she rounded the building.

Moments later, Andrea burst out the rear door, looking much livelier than she had yesterday. "I found some missing things after I cleaned Ricky's room," she called. "He took his sleeping bag and flashlight. They were there two days ago so that proves he's not hurt. Guess he just wants to be alone for a bit."

She stepped closer, searching Nikki's face for agreement. However, Nikki couldn't pretend to be relieved. Something had made Ricky run, something so frightening he didn't dare stay home. And someone had kicked out the window screen and ransacked his room. Left a strong message.

Andrea continued talking, still smiling. "So that proves he didn't have an accident on his bike. By the way, I haven't seen Cedro today. Hopefully he'll come by soon and you can talk to him."

"We already spoke," Nikki said. "But he couldn't tell me the company, or even Pope's last name. What do you know about the porta potty route? Or events they serviced?"

"Ricky never told me much," Andrea said, her smile not quite as bright.

"Would any of his friends know?"

"I'll check with them again. But Ricky isn't a big talker, even at home."

He may have shared more details with his classmates, Nikki thought. Even just to fill in some tedious school hours. She only needed one venue in order to find the porta potty company and track down Ricky's boss. The seven companies she'd already called had no record of Ricky Lopez's employment. The porta potty angle might prove to be a dead end. But it was one of the few threads she had to follow. That and Andrea's ex-boyfriend.

"Where did you meet Cedro?" she asked, careful to keep her voice casual, knowing Andrea was quick to turn defensive.

"At the track. He was coming by the kitchen, having coffee. We saw each other off and on. Nothing serious."

"Did you ever go to his place? Meet any of his friends?"

"No, he shares a dorm room so he always came to my apartment. He and Ricky get along good so we stayed friends. Cedro says Ricky was a lot like him when he was that age."

And then Cedro had found Ricky a job. The man must have some compelling reason to refuse to help a frantic mother and a kid who he apparently liked.

"So Ricky liked him coming around?" Nikki asked.

"Sure, he looked up to him." Andrea crossed her arms. "Like I said, Cedro never touched him. Not in an abusive way. Besides, Ricky never would have stood for it. He may not talk much but he's a fighter. So he has no reason to hide, if that's what you're thinking."

The fact that Ricky had sneaked into his house and gathered camping equipment showed he was certainly hiding from someone. His home life seemed uneventful. Andrea claimed they hadn't fought, and with her working early mornings and Ricky working after school, they seemed to have had little opportunity to argue.

Nikki rubbed her forehead. "Did he get along with his teachers? Any problems at school?"

"Just the normal. Sometimes he cut classes but that was because he wasn't learning anything. Then when he got the job, he was more interested in making money."

"What about his boss, Pope? Everything good there?"

"Ricky never complained. Seemed grateful to have the job. But the last couple weeks he was around the house more. Clammed up when I asked why he wasn't working."

"Talk to his friends again," Nikki urged. "See if you can find out any of the porta potty locations. Even the general area would help. Along with anything at all about Pope."

Andrea gave a slow nod. "All right. I'm off at three and will call then. But I think Ricky will be back soon. Even if it's only to get more food."

"Leave a note. Let him know you're worried and you just want him to come home. Tell him you love him and you're not angry and you can work out any issues together. Sometimes that's all kids need to hear."

"Sounds like you ran away before."

"More than once," Nikki said.

CHAPTER THIRTEEN

Nikki walked along the first floor of the grandstand, keeping Gunner out of the sun and in the relative coolness of the building. There was enough time to drop by the security office before heading to Sonja's. Hopefully Travis Hillman was around. He might be reluctant to give any personal information about Cedro but it would be interesting if he was known to security. The track generally had a good read on troublemakers.

Security at Santa Anita was definitely top notch. Video cameras had been installed throughout the grounds, from the shedrows to the backside entrances, with 24-hour monitoring. The goal was to protect the horses. But if a worker had a tendency to push the weaker around, or try to run a scam, Travis would know.

She shortened Gunner's leash as they approached the office. This was an important place for him to be obedient. She wondered if Travis would recognize her or if she'd have to pull out her creds. On the occasions they'd met, she'd been with Justin.

A woman leaned over the reception desk, complaining about a water truck's exhaust and how the fumes were affecting her horses. Seemed the driver said her horses were too slow to ever win, regardless if he shut off his engine. Judging by the heated conversation, it would be awhile before the matter was resolved.

"Need any help, Nikki?" a broad-shouldered man called from an open office door. Travis Hillman, Director of Security and Operations rose from behind his desk, motioning her inside with a welcoming sweep of his hand. Obviously he recognized her, or more likely it was Gunner that he remembered.

Travis waited for her to take a seat before settling back in his thick leather chair. "Is Justin here too?" he asked. "How's his new Barkeeper filly doing?"

"She's good. All the horses are training well," she said, appreciating his interest. He seemed to really love the animals. Next to the people, the horses' health was the most important. Jobs depended on it, including his. "I'm here hoping to get some background on a man named Cedro Rugger."

"Is he an exercise rider?" Travis shifted, turning to his computer and clacking keys. "They're subject to random drug and alcohol tests. But we can always request a voluntary one if Justin has reason to be concerned."

"No, he's with maintenance. I assume he works directly for the track. Just wondered if he's had problems with anyone."

Travis tilted his head, as if puzzled why she was worried about a maintenance worker. He didn't ask any more questions though, concentrating instead on his screen. It only took a few moments for him to pull up the information.

"I do have something," he said. "Disagreement in the rec hall, five months ago. Whacked a guy with his pool cue. One of our guards broke up the fight. A warning was issued. Nothing since but, as you know, the backstretch community likes to handle their own problems."

He swung around in his chair, his big arms folded over his chest. "Is Justin looking at this guy for something? Something off-track? I'd expect a courtesy call, considering we once worked together. But I guess anything Justin's involved with must be big?"

"It's nothing to do with him," she said, amused at how he seemed to idolize Justin. "This is my own investigation."

"Oh, that's right." He leaned back, relaxing, his bulk making the chair squeak. "I forgot you're a PI. So, is this guy cheating on his wife? Or maybe he's looking for another job and you're running a background check? I have to admit, I'm relieved it's nothing important."

Nothing important. She'd learned not to react to disparaging comments, at least when she needed someone's good will. Too often law enforcement types, especially men, assumed that her business consisted of domestic cases and employee checks.

Admittedly she did some of that to plump out her paycheck, but her specialty was missing persons. Nothing was more fulfilling than bringing someone home, especially a child. Being on the police consult list meant she and Gunner had participated in a variety of search and rescue ops, some of them high profile. It also meant she couldn't reveal any details about her work, or her contract.

"Guess you can't tell me why you're interested in this guy," Travis said, correctly picking up on her silence. "That's okay. Not our business. But from my point of view he doesn't seem like a dangerous dude, provided you don't play pool with him.

"And you do have that old dog." He gave a dismissive chuckle, barely looking at Gunner who was sprawled beside Nikki, eyes closed, relishing the air-conditioned office. "Even if his bark is worse than his bite."

Nikki squeezed the arms of her chair, irritated more by how he discounted Gunner than her PI business. But Gunner didn't need defending; he'd earned his accolades, even if this man was unaware.

"Let me know if I can be any more help," Travis said, rolling his chair back and rising to his feet. "And remind Justin he has an open invitation to drop by and see our video room. Over a thousand cameras watch the roads, barns and shedrows. A big investment but it ensures racing's integrity."

Nikki rose a bit reluctantly. She hadn't learned much about Cedro, and the video room was something she'd also like to see. Santa Anita was reputed to have the best security of any track in the country. Clearly though, her PI license didn't carry much clout. Travis's allegiance still belonged to the tight police fraternity.

Gunner's nails clicked on the tile as he scrambled to his feet, blinking sleepily. He would have preferred to stay longer too. It had been a warm and dusty walk from the barns to the security office, with little gained for the effort.

No matter. She subscribed to several databank services that provided addresses, contact info, relatives, and associates. She'd do her own digging on Cedro. Hopefully she'd turn up something more interesting than a swinging pool cue.

CHAPTER FOURTEEN

Nikki always enjoyed the drive to Sonja's, often cruising below the speed limit so she could absorb the view. Her friend's rescue ranch sat at the edge of the San Gabriel Mountains, a welcoming oasis of fresh air and freedom. This was the place where she and Gunner had honed their tracking skills, learned to trust each other and work as a team. It was also the retirement home of Stormy, the feisty pony who'd taught Nikki how to ride.

Stormy was still one of Gunner's favorite animals and he pressed his nose against the side window, as if aware of their destination. She wasn't sure if it was the scenery or unique smells, but he always seemed to know when they were within five miles of Sonja's acreage.

Obviously there wouldn't be any new critters to meet on this trip. Not only had Sonja suspended her psychic business, she'd also declined to accept any new animals. It was understandable she wanted to focus on helping her brother, but cutting off everything that gave her pleasure didn't seem healthy.

Nikki eased her car up Sonja's driveway, past a haughty-looking llama with a missing ear, and parked close to the wraparound porch. Sonja rose from her chair and rushed down the planked steps.

"Quick," she said, yanking open the driver's door. "Let's get Gunner in Liam's bedroom while he's still hiking."

"Some of this stuff needs to go in your freezer," Nikki said mildly. She stepped out, opened the hatch and passed Sonja two grocery bags. "And Gunner needs to stretch his legs first."

Sonja nodded but kept glancing at the trees, as if fearing Liam might emerge at any moment. She was so jittery that she fumbled the bags, sending oranges rolling over the dirt.

"Doesn't he usually stay out most of the afternoon?" Nikki asked, kneeling down and rescuing the fruit while Gunner trotted over to the closest tree. "Seems like a positive that he's enjoying nature again."

"That was my first thought. But these wilderness parks are all connected. He might find someone back there. If anyone can sniff out drugs, it's Liam. And there's little cell service if he runs into trouble."

"But he needs something to do in his day," Nikki said. "I don't think drug dealers do much business in the mountains."

"One would think." Sonja's voice thickened. "But that's not what I'm feeling. And any hiker could be carrying extra pain meds. Yesterday I followed him along that west trail by the canyon. Lost him where the trail splits. So I ordered an Apple tag that works off satellites. Once it comes, I'll sew it in his pack. Then I'll know everywhere he goes."

Nikki was on her knees reaching for a fallen orange, but now she paused, gaping up at her friend. Sonja wasn't moving on. If anything she was becoming more paranoid. If Liam needed that much supervision, he should have professional help.

"I'm not sure of the ethics—"

"Don't talk about ethics!" Sonja snapped. "My visions are telling me that those trails are dangerous. So I need to know what he's doing and where he's going, every minute of the day. I prefer a brother who hates me, to one who is dead and gone. You don't understand, you can't know..."

Sonja flinched, squeezing her eyes shut. "Guess you do know," she muttered. "So you'll understand why I'll do whatever it takes."

Gunner must have picked up on the tension. He loped back and shoved his head under Nikki's arm. Still kneeling, she set the oranges down and scratched his chest, knowing she and Sonja both needed a moment. A missing person was a unique hell, not knowing if a loved one was alive or dead. And like Sonja, she would have gone to extreme lengths to keep her safe.

She took several cleansing breaths then rose to her feet. "Ok, I'll grab Gunner's harness and see what he can find. And you don't have to wait for the Apple delivery. I have some tracking devices in the car. I'll show you how they work."

Sonja gave her a wordless nod then led the way into the house. She jammed the frozen goods in the freezer, left the rest of the food on the counter and headed down the hall. "Ricky is using the guest room on the left," she called. "Come on."

Nikki followed her into a familiar bedroom. She and Justin had spent many nights in this spacious room. It looked smaller now, with Ricky's belongings strewn on the bed, the chair and over the floor.

"I suspect he deliberately leaves this mess so he'll know if I was in here." Sonja gave a frustrated sigh. "It's hard to replace things exactly the same way. He's very crafty."

Or else he was just messy, Nikki thought. But she didn't speak, wanting to keep her focus on Gunner. He kept glancing up at her face, understanding the significance of his work harness and waiting for direction.

"Find," she said, unclipping his leash.

He shot forward, full of confidence. Leaped up on the bed, sniffed around the pillows and the headboard. Then he jumped down, checking over and around the wrinkled shirts and a scatter of underwear.

A running shoe in the closet grabbed his attention but only for a second. He trotted to the window, rose on his hind legs and sniffed at the ledge. Then he dropped back to the floor and stared at Nikki, his expression sheepish.

"There's nothing here," Nikki said. At least nothing he'd been trained to find. The practice tin contained a mixture of drugs, including fentanyl and cocaine. But if Liam was using something other than those drugs, Gunner wouldn't alert to it.

"Are you sure?" Sonja asked. "He didn't search for long. Tell him to check again."

Nikki wavered. She didn't like to question Gunner. It could create an insecure dog who alerted incorrectly, in an attempt to please. On the other hand, Gunner had only been training on drugs for a short time. It was possible he'd missed something.

"Find," she repeated sternly.

Gunner cocked his head, eyes puzzled. He circled around the room then ran from the bedroom and led them down the hall, his nails clicking excitedly on the wood floor. Then he stopped and scratched at the front door.

"The barn," Sonja said. "Bet Liam hides his stuff there. He pretends he's fixing bikes but he can just grab it, go for a hike and get high."

She swung open the door. Gunner charged past, across the verandah and down the steps. He didn't look at the barn. Instead, he ran directly toward the driveway, hot on a scent.

CHAPTER FIFTEEN

Gunner charged to Nikki's car and sat by the bumper, tail thumping the dirt. She swallowed a groan, knowing exactly what he'd alerted to. She shouldn't have ordered the second search. He was trying too hard, scrambling to find something that would make her happy. It was the same thing he'd done with the horse scent.

On a positive note, he had located drugs. And he deserved a reward.

"Good dog." She opened the door, pulled the drug tin from her pack, along with his ball. She played with him for several minutes, giving him her full attention before joining a disappointed Sonja who'd plunked herself back on the verandah.

"I appreciate all this," Sonja said, her words at odds with the irritated way she tapped the arms of the chair. "But that didn't help. I was certain he'd be able to find Liam's stash."

"Maybe Liam doesn't have a stash."

"But I can't shake the sense that something horrible is going to happen. I see drugs and mountains and death."

"So you're still having strong visions?"

"Only about Liam." Sonja squeezed her eyes shut. "And the knowledge that he's desperate for drugs and willing to do anything. If only Gunner had found something. Then I'd have an excuse to insist he not go on those long hikes."

Gunner *had* found something, Nikki thought, dropping onto the chair beside Sonja. And Liam's interest in exploring the wilderness might be a good thing. Hiking was a good way to clear one's head. Sonja might be so stressed about her brother that what she thought was a psychic vision was only an understandable fear of his relapse.

Maybe it would help Sonja to think about someone else. Someone like Ricky. On the other hand, Sonja had stopped working. She hadn't been in her office for over a month and had cancelled appearances at two prominent psychic fairs. Had made it clear she didn't want to think about horses or races or missing kids.

Besides, Sonja wasn't always right. Some of her visions had led Nikki down false trails. It did help to discuss cases with her though, since Sonja had a different approach than Justin. The two were polar opposites and their diverse opinions helped avoid tunnel vision. Something Nikki knew she was susceptible to.

She leaned forward, deciding she should at least mention Ricky. Sonja could help, or not.

"I'm currently looking for a twelve-year-old boy," Nikki said. "His mom thinks he's camping in the wilderness, about fifteen miles southwest of here."

"Can't Gunner find him?" There was a hint of snark in Sonja's voice.

"We don't have his entry point. He's familiar with both Bailey Canyon and Mount Wilson, and we suspect he's on a bike."

But Sonja only shrugged. She didn't ask any questions and her face remained morose. For someone who was usually quick to give an opinion, her disinterest emphasized how absorbed she was with her brother.

Nikki fingered the wooden armrests, fighting her irritation. Ricky needed help: He was only twelve.

A hundred feet away, Gunner happily nosed around Stormy's paddock, the pony following. It was much easier to have a dog as a partner. Gunner was always enthusiastic and never had mood swings. And though she didn't want to hurry off, she was wasting time sitting here. Liam didn't seem to be in any immediate danger. Ricky was another matter.

The boy was so scared he preferred to camp somewhere. The danger didn't seem related to school or his home life. It had to be work related. The job with Pope certainly seemed sketchy.

Sonja closed her eyes, obviously preferring silence, so Nikki pulled out her phone and logged onto her databank service. There were scores of Cedro Ruggers that came up on her screen, but only one who worked at Santa Anita Park. Age 34, married to Carmen Rugger. His work history didn't list a porta potty company and the Highland Park address was different than the track dorm.

Andrea said Cedro was divorced and lived on the backside but Travis Hillman had let it slip that Cedro was still married, according to track records. Maybe he was only separated and his wife still lived at the Highland Park address. She'd know quite a bit about Cedro, and estranged or divorced spouses were often enthusiastic about sharing details. Especially sordid ones.

"I gather you're leaving to look for that kid now," Sonja said, not opening her eyes.

Nikki wished it were that easy. She was still trying to establish why Ricky was hiding. At this point, it was like pulling at threads, hoping one would unravel.

"I'm just checking out an address," she said. "Trying to find his employer. I don't expect him to be there."

"Keep Gunner in the car," Sonja said. "Windows down."

"I don't have to lower the windows for him anymore. Had an air conditioning unit installed."

"I know that," Sonja said.

CHAPTER SIXTEEN

Nikki checked her GPS as she cruised through a residential area of Highland Park. Cedro's old address matched a yellow bungalow, the paint faded from the California sun. The front curtains were drawn, giving privacy along with protection from the heat. A rope was knotted around the front porch, thick enough to hold a small rhino.

It was difficult to tell if anyone was home. The adjacent house had a watering can lying beside a wilted flowerbed, but there was no movement and no sounds, other than the distant pop of a car backfiring. A couple of cars sat further down the street along with a newer model missing its hubcaps. Maybe Carmen Rugger didn't own a vehicle. She did have a dog, a big one judging by the size of that rope.

Nikki drove another thirty feet and parked two houses away. The big rope might only be for show but any dog would be protective of his property. No need to antagonize by having Gunner in sight.

"Stay," she said, reaching back and giving him a pat. This would likely be a quick visit. She paused then lowered the rear window. It'd be a waste of air conditioning but Sonja's cryptic comment about lowering the window was fresh in her mind. And easy enough to follow.

She walked toward the house and up the walkway. Was ten feet from the door when a series of booming barks reverberated. Definitely a big dog. A woman pulled the curtain back and peered out. Nikki gave a friendly wave and a moment later, the door opened a crack.

A massive pit bull rammed through the opening, her tail whipping in delight at the prospect of a visitor. She had to weigh almost a hundred pounds although she wasn't much higher than Nikki's knee.

"What do you want?" the woman asked, exhaling annoyance.

"What a beautiful girl," Nikki said, as the dog stopped barking and snuffled curiously at her legs. Compliments on pets and children were often the quickest way to start a conversation.

The woman appraised her dog with a critical eye. "I think she's ugly. But they guaranteed she'd attack if someone was aggressive."

"That's good," Nikki said, patting her broad head. The dog immediately flopped on her back, begging for a belly rub. And this was a good time to start asking questions. The woman couldn't close the door with the dog sprawled over the doorway. "Are you Carmen Rugger? Cedro's wife?"

"Who wants to know?" The woman's voice turned so cold that the dog scrambled to her feet, as if aware she should be doing something but was confused about the location of the threat.

Nikki passed the woman a business card, keeping the movement slow and unthreatening, conscious of the dog's sudden alertness. "My name is Nikki Drake. I'm a licensed PI looking for a missing boy, Ricky Lopez. His mother works at the Santa Anita track, same place as Cedro."

"We're not together anymore. Heard he's working over there but I don't want to know what he's done wrong."

"I'm not sure he's done anything wrong," Nikki said. But it was revealing that Carmen assumed her ex was involved in something shady. "He found Ricky a job. Cleaning portables for a man called Pope. I'm trying to find out Pope's last name along with the sanitation company he works for."

Carmen's face froze and she scooped her hand through the dog's collar, urging her inside. "I can't help. I don't know anything."

"Ricky's only twelve." Nikki eased her foot forward so the door couldn't close. "I just want to bring him home to his mother. That's all."

"You have to leave. Now."

The dog punctuated the woman's words with a throaty growl and Nikki knew she was running out of time. "Here's a picture," she said, holding out her phone. "Ricky on his bike, his mom behind him. He just wanted to make a little money."

"Doesn't everyone?" Carmen sounded bitter. But her eyes slid to the screen, interest sparking her face.

Nikki resisted the urge to keep talking, to say how Ricky hoped to save for a mountain bike but instead helped his mom buy groceries. Anything to stoke the woman's empathy. But sometimes it was best to wait, let silence do the work. Besides, Carmen had an imperious air and seemed like a woman accustomed to making her own decisions.

The dog whined, unsettled by the shifting emotions. Her tail was flattened, her ears back. She didn't know if Nikki was a welcome guest or not. It was often confusing for guard dogs that were trained for black and white situations.

"The mother is pretty, and very young," Carmen said, oblivious that her dog needed direction. "She must be worried about her son. But I don't know what Cedro is involved with. He's not welcome here, and now that I have this dog I don't have to worry about his visits. I do wonder if she's experienced his temper yet."

Nikki made an encouraging sound, hoping to keep her talking.

"He usually hides it from pretty ladies, especially at the beginning." Carmen pulled her eyes from the phone screen and studied Nikki. "Is he happy with this woman, do you think? Or did he hit on you too?"

Nikki laughed. "No, I can safely say we share a mutual dislike."

Something changed in Carmen's expression. She released the dog's collar and pushed the door welcoming wide.

"Come in," she said. "And I'll tell you all about my life with Cedro."

CHAPTER SEVENTEEN

"And that was the last time he hit me." Carmen grimaced over the mahogany coffee table. "We'd only been married six months before his fists started flying. He was volatile, always chasing a quick buck. Blaming me when the deals went south."

She rubbed her shoulder as if dealing with a nagging stiffness. "I ended up in the hospital a few times. He turned even nastier when I filed for divorce. I suspect he always had other women on the side and only married me because he wanted this place."

The part of the house that Nikki could see was strikingly plush and a contrast to its tired exterior. Walls had been removed to create a spacious living area filled with creamy leather furniture and subtle accent pieces. The modernized kitchen included a marble island and gleaming appliances. One of the coffee makers looked as complicated as a car engine.

Carmen had excellent taste and it was easy to imagine Cedro's bitterness at having to live in a backstretch dorm. Everything here was pristine, including the professionally framed pictures displayed on the mantle. There were no photos of any children and understandably not a single one of Cedro. Most of them included a solemn dark-haired man with a younger-looking Carmen.

"That's my father." Carmen's voice softened as she followed Nikki's gaze. "He died of cancer shortly after the wedding. He was the one who insisted Cedro sign a prenup. I thought it was unnecessary but Papi saw through his good looks. I might not be alive if he hadn't. Now my death won't benefit Cedro."

"You think he's capable of murder?"

"Maybe not when we first met, but he changed after doing jobs for Pope." Carmen gave a little shudder. "I never knew exactly what they were doing, but he turned mean. Ruthless."

"Were any of those jobs related to portables? To Santa Anita?"

"No. It surprised me when I heard he was working at the track. I assumed one had to like animals for that." Her shoulders dropped, her eyes shiny with contained tears. "And he's so cruel. I've seen him swerve to run over a cat or dog, and smile as he's doing it."

Nikki swallowed. "He's employed with the maintenance division. Fortunately he doesn't get too close to the horses." But she remembered Cedro's threats and realized they hadn't been bluster. He truly had no qualms about hurting a horse, and possibly a kid.

Carmen suddenly frowned, the lines around her mouth becoming prominent. "Just push Ginger away. Her hair flies everywhere. I prefer she stays outside but worry that Cedro might toss her something. I know he poisoned my neighbor's beagle."

Nikki folded her hands, aware she'd been patting the dog since she'd entered the house. But Ginger was hungry for affection and it appeared she didn't get much attention from her owner. Besides, the more she heard about Cedro, the more she despised him. And patting the dog helped keep her anger bottled.

"But the people Cedro hangs out with," Carmen went on, "would do much worse than toss poison."

"People like Pope?" Nikki asked. "What's his last name? Where I can find him?"

"Don't know. Never met him. Cedro just referred to him as Pope. But Cedro hoped if he could prove himself he'd get in tight with Pope's connections and finally make some real money."

"Did one of those connections own a sanitation company? Work with porta potties?"

"Is that what Pope's doing?" Carmen's lip curled with derision. "What a comedown. I never heard anything about toilets. Cedro made it sound like Pope was a big wheel, someone who could make people jump. I suspected they were involved in a car-theft ring but never knew for certain."

Nikki shifted, uncomfortable despite the soft leather of the sofa. If Pope was working with hardened criminals, it was possible Ricky had been sucked into a dangerous cesspool. Pope definitely seemed the key to finding the boy.

"Do you remember anything from Cedro's calls with Pope? Anything at all? Even something small might help."

"Sorry, Cedro was secretive, always going into another room. As if I cared!" Carmen flung her hands in the air. "The only time I heard anything was when he ran out of minutes and grabbed my phone."

"When was that?"

"About a year ago. But my call record won't help. Pope insisted on burner phones. And I don't remember what Cedro said. By that time, we didn't have much of a marriage."

Nikki tamped down her disappointment. Other than gaining a better picture of Cedro, this visit wasn't moving her any closer to finding Ricky's employer. "What about mutual friends? Anyone else who might know Pope?"

"No. I've moved on from Cedro and his scumbag friends. Doing well for myself and in a good place. But I do hope you find that boy." She tilted her head, suddenly thoughtful. "Maybe his mother had something to do with it. Maybe Cedro wants her but not her kid. He doesn't have much use for children."

Nikki was quite certain Andrea's distress was real, but that was an angle she hadn't discarded. However, she wasn't going to discuss the case with Carmen.

"Thanks for your help." She rose from the sofa, giving Ginger one last pat despite the flattening of Carmen's mouth. "Please call if you remember anything more about Pope. No matter how small."

Carmen nodded agreement but her eyes narrowed with disapproval. "Now there's brown hair all over the sofa, as well as your clothes. Your dog is going to wonder what you've been doing in here."

"You can tell I have a dog?"

"Saw him in your car on my camera. Was thinking there might be an entertaining dog fight. Ginger can be very ferocious if challenged."

Carmen sounded as if she might enjoy the brutality. And her dog followed Nikki to the door, as if willing to leave with a stranger.

"How long have you had her?" Nikki asked, hating to think of Ginger ending up in a fight ring.

Carmen paused, counting the days. "Almost nine months," she finally said. "Bought her from a guy who claimed she was professionally trained. I needed something to keep Cedro away in case he made an unwanted visit."

"Did it work?"

"Absolutely. I haven't seen him in ages. So it's worth putting up with a hairy dog."

Nikki fought an ache. Ginger was surely a physical deterrent but she only wanted to be loved. Unfortunately it didn't appear she'd ever receive much affection in this house.

CHAPTER EIGHTEEN

Nikki sat in her car after leaving Carmen's house, thinking about what she'd learned. No doubt about it, Pope was a dangerous man and somehow Ricky had become involved. Cedro knew more than he was saying but it would be difficult to make him talk.

Following Cedro was impractical, considering he lived at the track and even the most cautious surveillance would be noticed. She could tag his car and hope he might lead her to Pope, and Ricky. However, that was a circuitous and illegal process.

It would save a lot of time if there was a GPS tracker on Ricky. But while Sonja had ample chance to sew one in her brother's backpack, Ricky had already gathered his camping supplies. On the other hand, he might sneak back for more food. There were only so many berries he could pick, and his peanut butter must be getting low.

With that thought, Nikki turned her car and headed for the grocery store.

An hour later, she was in Andrea's kitchen, carefully wrapping a tracker in plastic and pushing it into the center of a newly purchased jar of peanut butter.

"If he comes back," Nikki asked, "what are the chances he'll grab this?"

"High," Andrea said. "Peanut butter is his favorite, whether it's in protein bars, cookies or sandwiches. Push that tracker right to the bottom though. We don't want him to find it too soon."

Nikki gave a conspiratorial grin, glad Andrea had embraced the tracker idea and was already pulling out a butter knife.

"I have some fresh rolls from the track," Andrea went on, taking the jar and expertly smoothing the top. "I'll leave those out too. Now he just has to come back and take them."

Hopefully Ricky wasn't too spooked to return. He might not know that his house had been broken into and his room tossed. But he seemed to understand he was in danger.

"I talked with Cedro's ex today," Nikki said. "She didn't know much about Pope either." In fact, even though Nikki had been there for almost half an hour, she hadn't learned anything concrete. Only that Cedro was abusive, and didn't like kids or animals.

Andrea nodded, busy wiping the edge of the knife with a dishcloth. "Cedro talks about her a bit. They're still friends even though he's the one who wanted the divorce."

Nikki twisted the peanut butter lid tighter. Cedro was a liar, claiming he'd been the one to do the leaving. Some people believed they were irresistible, and that spousal violence should be accepted.

"Tell me," she said then waited until Andrea had turned away from the sink. "Did Cedro ever do more than push you? I saw how he shoved you outside the kitchen."

"No. I already said he never hit me. And he certainly never harmed Ricky. They get along great."

But Cedro didn't like kids. Maybe he'd faked affection in order to stay in favor with Andrea. He certainly wasn't doing anything to help Ricky.

"I wonder why he won't tell us anything about Pope," Nikki said, watching Andrea's expression. "Or the porta potty job. Because for some reason it seems he doesn't want Ricky to be found."

Andrea turned and yanked open a drawer. Utensils clinked as she replaced the butter knife. "It's my fault," she muttered. "I should have paid more attention to where Ricky worked. That's a mother's job, not Cedro's."

Nikki felt some empathy but she had to push. It didn't help that Andrea worked long days, and waking hours with Ricky had been scarce. And right now Andrea seemed comfortable with this line of questioning.

"Maybe Cedro can still tell us something," Nikki said. "What kind of car does he drive?"

"Don't know the make. But it's blue, four door, with a track sticker on the windshield. I'll ask around."

"No need," Nikki said quickly, worried Cedro might hear about Andrea's sudden interest in his car. A man with his background would know why, and it wouldn't help if he started checking for a tracker. She'd obtain the information on her own. Track security would have a record.

It was after five though, and Travis Hillman wouldn't be back in the office until tomorrow. She didn't want to wait. It was almost dark and the perfect time to tag a vehicle when most workers would be relaxing in their dorms. Fortunately she had a few reliable sources in law enforcement who'd be open to running a plate.

And one of them was Justin.

CHAPTER NINETEEN

Justin answered on the fifth ring. "I'll be home in a couple hours," he said. "Have you eaten?"

"Not yet." Nikki pulled out from the curb fronting Andrea's house, straining to hear. Judging by the background sounds, Justin was in the office.

"I'll grab something for us on the way home." A door closed and Justin's voice turned clearer. "Press conference tomorrow so I'm going to stick around the house until noon. Do you have anywhere you have to be in the morning?"

"Travis Hillman's office. I need to get a license plate number for a track worker."

"And for that you'd miss out on bacon and eggs? And a back rub?"

"Not happily," Nikki said, moved by the deep promise in his voice. "But this is about the missing boy. He's still out there and Cedro isn't a savory character. He's the same punk who threatened our horses."

"What's his last name?"

"Rugger," Nikki said. "Cedro Rugger, male, early thirties."

A keyboard clicked. Moments later, Justin spoke again. "Nothing showing with a Santa Anita address. Got something that fits for Highland Park though."

"That's it." Cedro obviously hadn't updated his address. That might prove to be a mistake. Carmen was too bitter to be diligent about forwarding his mail.

"That's close to where I was earlier today," Justin said. "Scene I looked at for the narcotics task force."

"Were you able to help?" She shot a guilty look at her pack lying on the front seat. It had been a tremendous tool to have the drug sample but it was Justin who was making the payment.

"Hopefully." There was a rare weariness in his voice. "But it was bad. Fentanyl overdose, two adolescents dead. One of them was fourteen."

Nikki gripped the steering wheel, hating to hear about the loss of young lives. Hopefully Cedro's movements would help find Ricky, and his would be one life they could save.

"Got a plate, blue Toyota Corolla," Justin said, reading off a number. "So you're going to the track now? I imagine most track workers are in bed. Might be hard to talk."

"It's best to get this done tonight." She swung to the curb, grabbed a pencil and jotted down the plate number. It was an offence to attach an electronic tracker without permission and she didn't want to involve Justin. As a city detective, he played by the rules. She had more leeway, one of the many reasons she'd gone private.

"Then I won't have to hurry away tomorrow," she added. "You know, to talk to him."

Justin's sigh showed he knew exactly what she intended to do once she found Cedro's car. And it wasn't to talk. But he didn't probe or make gratuitous warnings about legality.

"Remember the cameras," was all he said.

CHAPTER TWENTY

The backside of the track was dark and sleepy, just as Nikki hoped. She strolled past several shedrows, keeping Gunner's leash short, her awareness of the surveillance sharpened by Justin's warning.

She already knew where most of the cameras were installed and could guess at the others. Barns were well covered but it was unlikely many had been placed by the staff parking lot. With any luck, she'd find Cedro's car there, and be able to tag it unseen.

Gunner veered, automatically heading to their shedrow. She changed direction too, deciding to give him a quick visit with Sugar. If anyone was watching, it would give her visit legitimacy.

They were twenty feet from their barn when an aggressive figure stepped from the shadows. Gunner's head lifted, his body language turning just as hostile.

"Good evening," she called to the security guard, cueing Gunner that everything was okay. He wasn't used to men blocking the entrance to what he considered his barn. Justin hadn't wasted any time hiring reinforcements and clearly had taken her warning about Cedro Rugger seriously.

"Hello," the man said, his shoulders relaxing. "I was told one of the owners had a German Shepherd. Everything is quiet tonight. You're the first person I've seen."

"I was in the area. Just wanted to check on the horses."

"Nothing to worry about." He gave a low chuckle. "These animals are video monitored, 24-7. It's a cushy job considering how many safeguards are in place. No one could get to a horse here."

The guard sounded as confident as Travis Hillman although the insignia on his uniform showed he was with a private firm. The improvements the industry had made were commendable, not only with testing but also with surveillance. She'd never been so aware of being watched and resisted the urge to wave.

Gunner had already discounted the guard and was pulling on the leash, impatient to see Sugar. The gelding was just as eager, his head stretched over the stall guard, ears pricked. He even let out a welcoming nicker.

"Obviously that's one of your horses," the guard said, following her down the aisle.

"He actually belongs to the trainer," she said. "But he's my dog's favorite." Truthfully Sugar was everyone's favorite. He was a real gentleman and still ranked one of the best stalls, even though he was no longer racing.

Last year, the trainer had taken Sugar home to his ranch and turned him out in a grassy pasture, thinking he deserved a leisurely life with fellow retirees. However, Sugar had missed not having a job. It turned out he enjoyed the track routine and excelled at teaching young horses how to behave.

Right now though, Sugar was acting oddly rude. He kept nudging at Nikki's backpack, almost knocking her sideways with the force of his head. She pushed him away, surprised by his behavior.

Then she understood. He was reacting to the drug sample in her pack. The repetitions with Gunner had left Sugar believing that the smell of drugs meant a peppermint.

"You're absolutely right, big guy," she said, digging in her pocket for a mint, wondering if it was time to leave the drug sample home. Its presence had proved confusing to both Gunner and Sugar.

"Hey, what are you doing?" The guard stepped in front of the stall, blocking her arm. "You can't feed him anything."

"It's just a peppermint." She opened her hand, letting the guard see the pink candy.

"Doesn't matter. Too many things can cause a positive test. And that's bad optics for racing."

"You're right," Nikki said, impressed with the guard's awareness. The trainer was fine with mints, and Sugar was no longer racing. But drug tests were so sensitive that horses nibbling the wrong blade of grass had become worrisome. Someone might have spilled a soft drink or dropped a tiny piece of chocolate, and that would be enough caffeine to show up in a random test. It was actually reassuring this guard was so vigilant, just in case Cedro was lurking.

She slipped the mint back in her pocket and scratched Sugar beneath his jaw. He tilted his head, enjoying the attention almost as much as a treat, ironically reinforcing his notion that the smell of drugs meant good things.

"I'm heading back to my car now," she said meekly. "Probably see you some other night."

The guard nodded, accompanying her to the front of the shedrow, apparently deciding she wasn't safe to leave alone. Trust Justin to find a conscientious security company.

She turned left, focused now on locating Cedro's car. He lived onsite so there was a good chance he'd park in the lot adjacent to the far end of the barns.

She headed toward the parking area in the south corner, picking her way over the dirt road. Darkness shrouded the barns, the road lamps casting an eerie glow but failing to light up the ruts. And all the talk of cameras left the back of her neck itching. She checked over her shoulder, unable to shake the feeling that she was being watched.

A horse slammed his stall wall, the sudden sound cracking like a rifle shot. Two more swift kicks followed. She peered in the direction of the ruckus, wondering what he was upset about and hoping he wouldn't hurt himself.

It was hard to see through the gloom. At least the horse had stopped kicking. Or maybe a groom had soothed him, although she couldn't see anyone. She turned her back to the overhead light, letting her vision adjust to the darkness, and finally caught a person's outline. A man stood motionless, likely checking on the noise. But grooms rarely had time to stand still.

She glanced at Gunner. Strange behavior always triggered his suspicions. He was oblivious though, staring straight ahead, not even looking in that direction.

Still, the man didn't move. And as her eyes adjusted to the dark, it was clear he was pointing at her, showing a second person her location. Her heart kicked and she rose on the balls of her feet, readying for a fight or flight. Then the clouds moved, moonlight broke through, and she recognized the figure for what it was.

Only a jockey statue.

She hadn't realized she'd quit breathing until it escaped in a whoosh. And she shook her head, annoyed at her odd jumpiness.

After all, the track was a safe place, with advanced surveillance and entrances manned twenty-four hours. She'd never thought much about the cameras. She also wasn't accustomed to it being so dead quiet. But more worrisome was Cedro's ex confirming that he was dangerous—to both animals and people.

She continued walking, reminding herself that their horses were safe, and that Gunner would alert to Cedro's presence. He'd met him twice before and both times the man had been aggressive. Gunner never forgot a threat.

Right now though, Gunner was relaxed at her side, content with his night walk. Probably the difference was that he didn't know someone in a security room was watching. She did. And she didn't like the feeling.

She swung to the left, choosing a narrow footpath that cut between the barns. It was almost pitch dark here but there were no cameras, and her tension eased. She placed a hand on Gunner's shoulders, using him as a guide, and he obligingly slowed his pace, as if understanding she depended on his night vision.

It was slow walking but worth a stumble to escape surveillance. Besides, the staff parking area was close. If she remembered correctly, there were only two shedrows and a maintenance building between her and the unofficial lot.

The path emerged at the side of a squat cinderblock building, the same maintenance building where she'd found Cedro yesterday. An overhead light from the adjacent shedrow spilled over the window, so she stopped and peered in.

At first it was all inky darkness. But when she shifted sideways, the light behind her revealed a row of metal shelves, crammed with paper towels and paint cans. It was hard to see the other end but there was no obvious sign of Ricky or his bike.

Something rustled in the grass, uncomfortably close to her feet. She wanted to think it was a cat, even though it was probably a rodent considering Gunner's low growl. He liked cats but abhorred rats, and there were plenty of those living around the barns. Horses dropped a lot of grain from their buckets, and rats were drawn to easy pickings.

"Leave it," she murmured.

"Did you hear that?" a woman asked. Nikki's heart slammed against her ribs, shocked by the voice coming from behind the wall.

She dropped below the window, at the same time tapping Gunner's nose, warning him to stay quiet. But she recognized that voice and the knowledge filled her with disbelief, and anger.

"It's nothing," Cedro muttered. "Don't stop."

"But I heard something."

"You're so good, babe. Keep sucking."

Andrea and Cedro. Together. And Andrea sounded like an enthusiastic participant. Why had she lied about their relationship? Did that mean she hadn't been honest about her son?

Nikki's stomach roiled, her emotions leaving her nauseous. She didn't want to listen while they had sex but they might say something about Ricky. And her anger with his mother flattened any concerns about propriety.

She eased onto the ground, finding a comfortable position below the window sill. She might be here awhile. It was obvious from Cedro's groans that he was having a very good time. And post-coital talk could be invaluable.

She scratched Gunner's chest, blocking the unwanted images, letting her dog know everything was fine. Even though it wasn't.

CHAPTER TWENTY-ONE

Nikki heard Cedro's satisfied grunt. Then the clink of a belt buckle. "Let's go," he said.

That was fast and disappointing, for both Andrea and Nikki. There had been no intimate lovers' talk. No talk at all. Nikki scrambled to her feet and tiptoed to the side of the adjacent barn, pulling Gunner into the darkened corner.

Moments later, Cedro appeared in the doorway, glancing around while he tightened his belt. He turned and motioned. Andrea appeared by his side, her slim figure almost hidden by his shoulders. They didn't speak, just headed down the road toward the parking lot.

Probably driving her home, Nikki decided, keeping a hand on Gunner's collar. He was tracking Cedro with his ears, his body rigid. This had been the third time he'd encountered the man and he'd rightly slotted Cedro as a non-friend.

She didn't dare follow. Gunner's silhouette would be too distinct. Worse, Cedro probably knew now that she'd been asking about his car. Her hands clenched, her nails digging into her palms. Andrea was Ricky's mother: the person who was supposed to protect him. Not betray.

"Heel, Gunner," Nikki whispered, turning and hurrying in the other direction. She needed her car and unfortunately she'd parked too far away to follow. On the other hand, their destination seemed obvious.

Twenty-five minutes later, she was rolling down Andrea's street. A blue Corolla was parked by the curb. It had to be Cedro's car.

She drove past another four houses before pulling to the curb and parking in a spot sheltered by a boxy van. The license plate Justin had provided was a perfect match. Jamming on a ball cap, she pulled the tracker from her pack and headed toward his car.

The sidewalk was deserted and several of the street lamps were broken, lending a welcome darkness. She strode along the sidewalk, keeping an eye on the front of Andrea's house. A figure shifted behind the curtains as if moving toward the door. She lengthened her stride, hoping there'd be enough time.

Just beside the rear of Cedro's car, she stooped, pretending to tie her shoe. Then she reached up and attached the magnetized tracker to the inside wheel well. Stood up and continued walking.

Moments later the front door opened, accompanied by the murmur of voices. She continued in the opposite direction, but couldn't resist peeking over her shoulder.

Cedro's head dipped as he gave Andrea an affectionate kiss. He lingered, clearly discussing something and in much less of a hurry than he'd been at the track. She was tempted to circle back and listen but the street was too deserted to remain unnoticed.

She turned right at the next block, walked a few feet then stopped. Cedro was heading toward his car. He waved at Andrea as if they were best buds before disappearing into his car and roaring away. His muffler obviously needed replacing. If he was still involved in a car theft ring, he wasn't keeping any nice vehicles for himself.

She pulled in a frustrated breath, tempted to climb the steps and confront Andrea. But the smarter strategy might be to pretend she had no inkling they were still tight. She had to believe Ricky was okay and that it was a good sign Andrea and Cedro had stopped arguing. Surely Andrea wouldn't be so friendly if she feared for her son's life. At least now there was a tracker on Cedro's car. He might be headed to Ricky's location tonight.

She jogged back to her car and opened up her tracking app, watching Cedro's route with hope followed by a growing disappointment. He seemed to be driving back to the track. She kept the screen open, ready to follow if he changed direction. But it was clear he was headed home.

Nikki glanced back at the house but the window was already dark. Andrea would be tired for her early start at the kitchen. Likely she wouldn't be prepared to answer tough questions. But tomorrow Nikki intended to find out exactly how truthful the woman really was.

Andrea had lied about Cedro. She may have lied about other things too.

CHAPTER TWENTY-TWO

"I didn't expect a home-cooked meal tonight," Nikki said, setting plates on the outdoor table while Justin expertly grilled the steak. Clouds had moved in, leaving their fence barely visible, but patio lights outlined the barbecue and dining area, making it feel like a private oasis.

It was fortunate she hadn't stayed and confronted Andrea. Justin was an excellent cook and she wouldn't have wanted to miss his effort, especially since it was supposed to be her job this month. The fact that he wanted to be outside also showed he'd had a tough day.

"Vinny's was a fifty-minute wait," Justin said. "Cooking was faster."

His food order would have been much quicker if he'd given Vinny's staff his name, but Justin was scrupulously fair. He was still paying back his favor to the task force, and one crime scene had turned into three. Whatever he'd seen today had left him needing an escape.

She twisted the corner of a napkin, grateful for the drug sample but regretting that it had created so much work. Along with the accompanying anguish.

"How many scenes do they want your help with?" she asked. "Thought it was only one?"

Justin bent and pressed a kiss against her cheek. "This is way past working off any favor. There were two more deaths today. Those kids had no clue what they were ingesting. I want to stop it."

The steel in his voice was unmistakable and when he straightened, the outside lights spotlighted the set of his jaw. "Whoever is lacing these drugs is a stone-cold killer," he said. "With no regard for lives."

The smell of sizzling steak filled the air but her appetite had disappeared. Youth were especially vulnerable to street drugs, looking for a cheap deal without much thought to its quality. But buying product laced with contaminants could be a death sentence.

"That's the same thing that happened to Sonja's brother," she said. "Only he was found in time."

"These teens were at a school football game, security guards at every gate." Justin jabbed the meat with such force that flames rose, fed by the escaping juice. "No description of the dealer since the girl who bought it didn't make it out of the hospital."

Nikki pushed aside the mangled napkin. Security was tight at school events so whoever carried drugs onto the grounds was taking a risk. But the bigger problem was further up the distribution chain where someone was cutting it with contaminants, increasing potency and profit. No doubt they lacked a chemistry degree, as well as a conscience.

Gunner trotted across the patio and rested his head on Nikki's lap, sensing her distress.

"How's his training going?" Justin asked, cutting off a piece of steak and setting it aside to cool. "Did he find anything at Sonja's?"

"Only the sample in my car. But I don't think there was anything on her property. I'm sure there wasn't," she added, needing to show faith in her dog. "So if you want his help with a drug scene, let me know."

"Not necessary. Two K9 teams are already assigned. Youth overdoses tend to get extra attention."

She nodded, tamping down her disappointment that she wouldn't have a chance to assist. Anyway, her spare time was limited. She had her own twelve-year-old to help. Hopefully Cedro's movements would lead her to Pope and he wouldn't check for a tracker. If he did, it would be because the duplicitous Andrea had warned him about Nikki's interest in his car.

Justin passed her the piece of cooled steak and she absently tossed it to Gunner, her mind jumping back to Andrea and tonight's sexual liaison. She didn't want to believe the woman was involved in Ricky's disappearance, that she'd sacrifice her son's wellbeing for Cedro. But facts couldn't be denied.

Nikki looked at Justin, her smile bleak. "People do despicable things for love or money, don't they?"

"All the time," he said.

CHAPTER TWENTY-THREE

Nikki's phone pinged from the bed table, jerking her from a deep sleep. She eased out from beneath Justin's heavy arm and checked her screen. The phone was set on do not disturb until 6 am but she'd been hoping to sleep later than that, especially considering Justin was taking a rare morning off. It had better be an emergency call, she thought, already missing the comfort of his body.

But it wasn't a call or text. Only her app noting that tracker 64 had been in motion—Cedro. And the time of his car drive was baffling. He'd left the track at four-thirty am, returning just before six. Now he was already back at his dorm. The man hadn't enjoyed much sleep following his blow job from Andrea. And Nikki didn't feel one drop of sympathy.

"Important?" Justin murmured, ever alert.

"Possibly," she said, still studying Cedro's route. He'd visited a spot bordering the wilderness park. With any luck, the location had something to do with Ricky. "I should go and check out this address."

"Could it wait a bit?" Justin slid a suggestive hand over her hip.

"Maybe ten minutes," she said, slipping back beneath the sheet.

Justin's chuckle was deep and full of promise. "I'm going to want a little more time than that."

She wanted more time too, and it was almost an hour later when she reluctantly pried herself from his arms and left the house.

Using her app, she retraced the route Cedro had taken. Gunner sat in the back of the car, watching through the side window, not as bothered as she was about missing leisure time with Justin, or a gourmet breakfast.

That was another bonus about having a dog as her partner. Gunner was never grumpy about a change in plans. Actually Justin had been equally unfazed, understandable since he was usually the one called away. Besides, she'd left him wearing a satisfied grin that might last all the way to his press conference.

He also hadn't questioned her use of a tracking device. Seemed her rule-compliant detective was softening, at least as far as her investigative tactics were concerned. Of course, he understood her motivations, had known her family back when they'd been desperately searching for a loved one.

She angled around a rut in the blacktop, checking the address. A few more miles. The property was registered to a numbered company, no mention of anyone called Pope. Maybe Cedro and Pope were keeping Ricky there, somehow influencing him to stay. After she checked out this address, she'd go to the track and ask Andrea some hard questions. Figure out her true relationship with Cedro.

Nikki swung around another hole in the pockmarked pavement, her mind churning out possibilities. Maybe it wasn't all sinister. Maybe Ricky had found his home life intolerable. Maybe someone had been abusing him, and his mother hadn't helped, so he'd chosen to stay with Pope. It was hard to accept anything Andrea said, now that she'd been caught in one lie.

Nikki turned down a rutted driveway flanked by oaks and softwood. The faded beware of dog sign was barely legible but a boulder had been freshly painted in red: Keep out.

Cedro had ignored the warnings so she did as well. She had a variety of cover stories prepared for situations like these, but sometimes it was best to wing it. Whom she would find at the end of the driveway was still a mystery. Hopefully it would include Ricky.

She rounded the last bend onto a patchwork of wizened grass fronting a white stucco bungalow. There was ample turnaround space but no vehicles, only a blue ATV parked by the trees. Judging by the complacent sparrows perched on the seat, it hadn't been used recently.

She slowed in front of the house then saw the damaged door and cranked her car around, readying for a quick exit. Someone had been here before her. Someone violent. The door was flattened, its hinges dangling from a splintered frame.

Cedro's work? He was strong enough to kick a door in.

She lowered her rear window. Gunner stuck his head out, nose lifted in the breeze, but he wasn't alarmed. And no one peered out the window. The only sound was the cheerful chirping of birds.

She tucked her phone and pepper spray into her pockets, stepped out and opened Gunner's rear door.

He jumped out, nose dropping to the ground. Seconds later, his lip curled. But he didn't growl, maybe because Cedro's scent was hours old. His hackles didn't lift either, reinforcing her sense that the place was empty.

Reassured, she climbed the three steps and called out a greeting. The only answer was the buzz of flies, delighted by the easy entrance.

There wasn't much to see beyond the flattened door. A short hallway led to the kitchen giving a partial view of a mustard-colored fridge. None of the other rooms were visible but other than rank food odors, there was nothing alarming.

Unlike police, private investigators didn't have special rights. However, Cedro obviously hadn't called the authorities requesting a wellness check, and any law-abiding citizen should be concerned about a broken door, and aiding a vulnerable occupant.

"Do you hear someone calling for help?" She looked at Gunner, who cocked his head, eyes grave.

"Me too." Brushing away the cloud of flies, she stepped over the downed door and into the house.

CHAPTER TWENTY-FOUR

"Hello," Nikki called. "Ricky, are you in here?"

She stopped in the hall, waiting for her eyes to adjust to the muted light and listening for movement. Outside, birds called but inside the bungalow there was only silence.

She headed toward the kitchen with Gunner beside her. Then she quickly raised her hand, motioning for him to stop. The place was a mess. Glass littered the linoleum floor, cupboard doors had been ripped off and ants paraded in a line, feasting on indistinguishable spills on the counter. Something brown skittered beneath the oven, and she jerked in revulsion.

Gunner growled, his attention locked on the base of the oven. Probably a rat, but if that was the scariest thing in here, there was little to worry about. She scanned the kitchen, keeping a hand on his collar, concerned about the glass shards and debating if she should go back to the car and grab his protective boots.

The glass was only in the kitchen though where someone had emptied a cupboard, knocking plates and glasses to the floor. The room was stripped of anything personal. There wasn't even a fridge magnet holding clippings in place.

Ironically the back door was unlocked. Whoever had kicked in the front door could have circled around and saved some effort. Unless they were in a hurry, or determined to make a point.

She checked the adjoining room. There was little furniture other than a TV, an end table and a stained sofa. The table drawer had been pulled out and upended, leaving no sign of mail or electronic devices. Nothing to provide any information about the occupant.

The bathroom and bedrooms were equally stark. Only the larger bedroom contained a bed. She pushed the closet door open with her foot but it was empty of anything but rodent droppings. Neither of the other two bedrooms showed any sign of occupancy, by Ricky or anyone else.

Why did Cedro come here? And what did he do? He'd only been here for a few minutes and certainly hadn't had time to break in and ransack the place. That had happened days ago, long enough for rodents to become comfortable. But something had motivated him to drive here so early in the morning. And the visit had occurred almost immediately after last night's booty call with Andrea.

With some digging, the principals of the numbered company could be established, but the real occupant might be tougher to determine. And even harder to find, especially if it was the elusive Pope.

She stepped outside, drawing in a cleansing breath. Despite the open door, the air in the bungalow was rank, smelling of rotting food and a dirty bathroom.

She circled the bungalow. No sign of any portable toilets, only sun-dried grass and the deserted ATV with an adult-sized helmet hanging from the bars.

She headed toward the four wheeler but even from a distance, it was obvious the license plate had been removed. The sparrows waited until she was ten feet from the four wheeler before flying away. She checked the wheel well, searching for the VIN, but the numbers had been scratched, leaving them unreadable.

The occupant had cleaned up well. Surprising he'd left such an expensive machine, unless he'd been forced to leave in a hurry. And Cedro hadn't stayed long, as if spooked by what he'd discovered. Or what he knew had happened.

A shiver ran down her neck and she wheeled, studying the property with narrowed eyes. A dirt trail led into the mountains. Other than that, there was only an overgrown game trail that showed no sign of human passage. Or of a body being dragged.

She checked the wider dirt trail, noting broken branches and tracks too big for an ATV. It was hard to guess how recently the vehicle had passed but she was curious to see where it had driven, and why. The trail should be moderately easy walking, more of a fire road than a four-wheeler trail.

Gunner had been sniffing at the shaded side of the house but he bounded to the car when she called, wagging his tail when she slipped on his harness and the tracking lead.

She tightened her backpack then returned to the four wheeler, picked up the helmet and held the cushioned padding in front of him. He sniffed it, his nose moist and quivering.

"Find," she said.

CHAPTER TWENTY-FIVE

Gunner clearly had a scent. Nikki kept a tight grip of his lead as he charged across the dirt clearing and up the trail.

"Easy," she called, working to keep pace. She hadn't expected him to find such a strong scent. He wasn't even sniffing the ground, but had his head in the air, running with purpose.

There was a steep drop on her right and she gave a little tug on the leash, asking him to steady. They were barely a quarter mile from the bungalow but she didn't want him scrambling into a ravine, didn't know what they might face. And she had an uncomfortable feeling this might not end well.

The tire depressions disappeared as the dirt changed to rock. But several dislodged rocks showed the vehicle had driven this way. Her uneasiness grew and she scanned both sides of the trail. She considered going back for her gun but Gunner was fixated on the scent, and it wasn't good to pull him off.

Minutes later she realized she didn't have to worry about confronting the truck occupants. There was an obvious spot where the truck had backed into the brush and turned, leaving a disturbance of rocks and chaparral. Something flashed in the corner of her eye and she jerked sideways, still on edge. But it wasn't human, only a coyote, its color blending against the grayish brown rock. No, not one coyote, but two that quickly turned into three.

"Get!" She waved an arm, pulling on Gunner's leash to stop. She wasn't unduly concerned but knew she shouldn't keep running, looking and acting like prey. However, Gunner was already sitting, his attention focused on the bottom of the ravine.

A breeze swirled upward, carrying the coppery smell of blood. And she forgot about the coyotes. Could only stare in horror at the ravaged body lying ten feet below. Please, not Ricky!

She swallowed, forcing her feet closer to the edge, trying to estimate the body's length. Predators had been freely scavenging and ripped clothing was scattered around the rocks, but the bulk of the body was still attached. She let out a sigh when she realized it was much longer than Ricky's five feet. The head and groin were mutilated but she was confident it was an adult male. At least he could be given a proper burial, thanks to Gunner. And she'd forgotten to reward him.

Good dog!" she said, giving him a pat. But she remained standing, conscious of the coyotes and the need to look big. Gunner didn't even ask for his ball. All his attention had switched to the lurking coyotes. His hackles were up, his growls loud and menacing now that his tracking job was done.

She pulled out her phone and pepper spray, keeping a careful watch. She didn't want the coyotes to tear up the body any more but she also didn't want Gunner to be drawn into an unnecessary fight.

They weren't moving closer though. In fact, only two were visible now. The bigger one was the last to slink away, resigned to giving up his meal. Evidently their bellies were already full.

Only one bar showed on her phone but when she climbed a rock and held it in the air, coverage increased. She pressed 911 and reported the grisly discovery, careful to add that she was a licensed PI with a tracking dog on a leash and a registered gun locked in her car.

Then she waited.

CHAPTER TWENTY-SIX

"And why did you drive onto the property?" the detective asked. "If you don't know the identity of the owner?"

"I'm investigating a missing boy," Nikki said. "This address came up through his mom as one he may have visited."

The woman had introduced herself as Detective Wilson, no first name given. "The power of parental tracking," the detective said, closing her notebook with an air of finality. "Everyone has 'Find Me' on their phone."

Not Ricky, Nikki thought, happy she didn't have to admit she'd relied on an illegal tracking app. But other than taking her contact information, Detective Wilson seemed uninterested in anything she had to say. The detective was equally unimpressed with Nikki's PI license.

"I'd appreciate it if you'd let me know the identity of the deceased," Nikki said. "And if he was the owner of the property. It might be related to my case. He definitely had driven the four-wheeler. My dog tracked him through the helmet."

The detective sniffed. "You're claiming your dog can track an ATV? Not even our trained K9s can do that. And the four wheeler wasn't near the body."

Nikki tried to ignore the detective's tone, along with the fact that she wasn't even listening.

"No," Nikki said. "I showed him the helmet. Then he followed the air scent. There are tire tracks so likely the body was dumped."

"Or he fell. But we'll figure it out. And the dead man's identity will be made public in due course."

Nikki pressed her lips together. Clearly there'd be no courtesy call. Some police worked well with private investigators. Not this one. "Maybe you missed the part where I'm looking for a lost boy?" she said.

"We don't release classified information to lay people," Detective Wilson snapped. "That includes private investigators. I suggest the parents file a report with the police. A missing child should be taken seriously."

"A report was filed about Ricky Lopez. It didn't prompt much action. And I am serious about my work." Nikki wanted to add that Gunner was a trained K9 but the detective had already turned away. And she was too annoyed to grovel.

On the other hand, they were all working toward the same goal. If the police were more interested in finding Ricky, it would only help.

She sucked in a breath, trying for a conciliatory tone. "Ricky worked after school for a man called Pope," she said. "Cleaning portables. If this address and the deceased are connected, it could have ramifications for the boy's disappearance. Cedro Rugger, a Santa Anita track employee, might know more. He found Ricky the job."

The detective's shoulders rose in visible annoyance but at least she'd stopped and turned. "What's Pope's full name?"

"Don't know. I was hoping to learn that from my visit here."

"And instead you found a dead body. Cause of death to be determined."

"The ravine wasn't that deep." Nikki grabbed the opening and stepped closer. "It certainly appears like a homicide, considering the break-in. Like you pointed out, the deceased didn't drive the ATV. And he didn't walk. The scent was all air."

Detective Wilson made a dismissive sound but at least she was listening. Hopefully she'd push the ID if an adolescent was involved. Nikki doubted she'd receive a call from the detective but anything to help Ricky would be welcome. Police attention would also put heat on Cedro and Andrea.

"You might be able to pull a quick ID off the four wheeler," Nikki said, aware of the technicians around the bungalow. They'd finished taking photos of her tires and seemed to be moving toward the trail. They hadn't even looked at the ATV.

"The VIN on the frame was scratched out," she added. "But often there's a hidden one."

"We don't need anything more from you," Detective Wilson said, her voice chilly. "This isn't the first call we've received because someone's pet was playing in the woods and stumbled over a body."

"My dog wasn't playing. He was following the scent on the helmet. It belonged to the dead man."

"Most any dog would have been attracted to that corpse."

"He's not just any dog. He's had K9 training and is certified for search and rescue."

The detective arched a thinly plucked eyebrow that went well with her sneer. "If he's that good, I'm surprised you're not on our consult list."

"We are."

For a split second, Detective Wilson looked surprised. Then her expression turned to the stony one that Justin had perfected. "Well, it was fortunate you visited today," she said, pulling out her notepad and penciling a notation. "Another week and there wouldn't have been much left. No one would have even known he was dead."

The killer knows, Nikki thought, concern banding around her chest. Hopefully Detective Wilson would push the ID, along with the autopsy. Because if that mangled body turned out to be Pope, it didn't bode well for Ricky.

CHAPTER TWENTY-SEVEN

The sun was almost overhead when Nikki pulled into the Santa Anita parking lot and exited her car. Heat rose in waves from the blacktop and most owners had left after morning workouts. At this hour, Andrea shouldn't be too busy in the kitchen. She'd have no excuse to avoid Nikki's questions.

A white SUV slowed beside her and the driver's window whirred down.

"Good morning, Nikki," Travis Hillman said. "You're late. Training hours are over and I'm heading out. Or did you need to see me again?"

"No, just visiting the horses."

"Good. Glad you're not here to run another employee check. We're already short of maintenance workers and with that last guy gone, it's really tight."

"That last guy? You mean Cedro Rugger?"

"Yes, he quit this morning. Walked out. Left the tractor and harrows in front of the starting gate. One of the horses almost ran into it. I assume you had something to do with his hasty departure?"

Dammit. She needed to talk to Cedro. So did the police. And now he was in the wind.

"Guess he got that job you were vetting him for?" Travis went on, drumming his fingers on the wheel, obviously in a hurry.

Gunner jerked at his leash, moving aggressively close to SUV.

"Sorry," Nikki said, tugging him back.

"No problem." Travis shrugged but frown lines bracketed his mouth. "Remember not to take him by the rail. And you can't be using the backside as a dog park, even at night. People have complained."

The cameras. She'd tried to avoid them last night but evidently she'd been seen. Still, no one had been disturbed and all the horses had been safe in their stalls. She hadn't even met anyone except for the private guard.

She wondered who'd complained but Travis wore that stern cop look, as if he were re-considering Gunner's entire presence. Unfortunately law enforcement types often required sucking up. She'd been trying to improve that skill but after her encounter with the detective this morning, her patience was frayed. A bit of name dropping might work though and she already knew Travis had considerable respect for Justin.

"Gunner's always on a leash." She forced her best smile. "And I keep him away from the horses. He's also had extensive training. Justin can vouch for his K9 background."

Travis had seemed to be in a hurry but now he shifted, resting his arm over the door and peering at Gunner. "That dog is a trained K9? He's so quiet. Thought I saw papers that he was a therapy dog?"

Nikki shrugged. In her mind, all dogs were therapy dogs; most weren't certified. "Yes, but Justin gave Gunner to me for my PI job. He's very versatile. And he has a great nose."

"Well, there's plenty to smell around here." Travis straightened, shifting his vehicle into gear. "Let me know if I can help with any more employees."

He hadn't been that much help, Nikki thought, but obviously Travis wanted to please Justin. And that worked for her, especially if it gave Gunner track privileges. She gave a cheery wave as he drove toward the exit then she pulled out her phone and checked her tracking app.

A blinking light showed Cedro's car was parked in a different spot from last night but still on the grounds. No doubt he wanted his car closer to the dorms so he could gather his belongings. Possibly what he'd seen at the bungalow had scared him so badly that he wanted to disappear. And her persistent band of worry tightened a notch.

She quickened her stride, almost jogging to the parking lot, relieved when she spotted Cedro's Toyota jammed next to a motorcycle. This wasn't even an official lot, just a spot at the back of the barns where workers left their vehicles. The track probably turned a blind eye, especially since there were no equine paths close by, and no horses to startle.

She rounded the back of the motorcycle and squeezed alongside Cedro's car. It looked different in the light, a sun-bleached blue with a nasty dent in the driver's door. The rear windows were tinted and impossible to see past, so she moved to the front and peered over the top of the windshield.

There wasn't much to see. The car was surprisingly empty, except for a torn racing program and a bag of dog treats lying on the passenger seat. She shook her head in disgust. Luckily Gunner was trained not to eat random food. If those treats were poisoned, there was no need to worry. And she'd already learned the private security firm watching the horses was diligent about food.

She straightened, relieved Cedro would no longer be allowed on the backstretch. It was an uncomfortable feeling knowing someone was willing to hurt an innocent animal. But if he was moving out, he hadn't loaded up his car yet so hopefully she could find him and try another round of questions. If not, at least his car was tagged.

A tracker simplified things, showing where a suspect was going and where he'd been. It probably wasn't a coincidence he'd quit following his pre-dawn drive. The smashed door and cleansing of the bungalow seemed to have left him surprised. And alarmed.

Likely he hadn't even seen the body. He'd been there for less than five minutes, not long enough to walk up the trail, find a coyote-ravaged corpse, and return to his car. The police had taken fifteen minutes to hike in.

She squared her shoulders, determined to learn more about Cedro and Andrea's relationship. If the body proved to be Pope's, maybe someone higher up was calling the shots, and Cedro had little input. Maybe he really didn't know where Ricky was, and had clammed up out of fear. The fact that Pope would likely be identified as the victim confirmed that Cedro should be scared.

It also validated Nikki's belief in the dead man's link to Ricky.

CHAPTER TWENTY-EIGHT

The tantalizing smell of bacon filled the air. Nikki left Gunner in his familiar spot beneath a shady oak tree and walked inside the track kitchen.

Justin's farrier, a garrulous man with a wealth of knowledge about lameness, called out a greeting. Usually she enjoyed having a coffee and learning from his experience, but today she gave him a quick hello and swept past, intent on finding Andrea.

She spotted her almost immediately. Andrea was bent over an empty table, a moist cloth in one hand, a spray bottle in the other. She looked up, her eyes widening when she saw Nikki.

"No time to talk," she whispered, bending back down and scrubbing at the pristine tabletop. It was notable she didn't ask if there was new information about her son.

Nikki's jaw tightened. People lied. In her line of work, it happened often. But this woman—a mother!—seemed to be colluding with Cedro at her son's expense. And that left Nikki horrified, and furious.

"Then make time," Nikki snapped.

"Can't. Someone will s-see." Andrea's voice was reed thin. It was then Nikki noticed the spray bottle was shaking. Actually the woman's entire body was trembling. Was she that afraid?

Nikki scooped up a menu, staring at the laminated sheet and list of specials. "I'll go now," she murmured. "But only if you text me. Give a spot to meet. And the meeting needs to be within the hour."

Andrea's nod was barely perceptible but it was there. Nikki moved up to the counter, bought a coffee and walked out, not giving Andrea a second glance.

Gunner rose, wagging his tail, delighted to see her emerge from the building so quickly. She gave him an absent pat and untied his leash.

Clearly Andrea didn't want to be seen talking to her. The app showed Cedro's car hadn't moved. Even though he'd quit his job, he might be hanging around. Was he watching Andrea? Is that why she was so spooked? They'd certainly been close last night.

Shaking her head, she headed toward Justin's shedrow, all the while keeping an eye out for Cedro. But if the man didn't want to be seen, he'd be difficult to spot. There were too many barns and nooks and crannies. And a worker like Cedro would know them all.

She had up to an hour to kill before her meeting with Andrea. She might as well use the time working on Gunner's drug training. Ricky's mother might not want her help but Sonja still did.

It was quiet enough to pull out the sample tin. Races were scheduled for that afternoon but her trainer didn't have any entries. A few grooms hurrying past might be a good thing, providing Gunner with some distractions. As long as she kept him leashed, Travis Hillman shouldn't mind. Just in case though, she'd work behind the barn where there was no camera coverage.

Sugar's welcoming nicker rang out as soon as they approached the shedrow. Colleen was hosing the horse down, sluicing water over his back and washing off the soap suds.

Sugar abruptly twisted, almost knocking the sweat scraper from her hand. "Stop," Colleen said, straightening him before throwing a welcoming smile at Nikki. "Is that coffee for me?"

"It is," Nikki said, carefully setting it down beside a giant bottle of shampoo.

"Good thing I'm almost finished," Colleen said. "He's sure excited to see your dog."

But Sugar stretched his neck out, reaching past Gunner to sniff at Nikki's backpack. Then he looked at Nikki with an air of expectation.

"Busted." Nikki smiled and pulled out a peppermint, letting Sugar lip the mint from her hand. "He was around for Gunner's scent training a few days ago," she admitted. "He's caught on as fast as Gunner. Maybe faster."

"What's the scent?" Colleen asked.

"Just some training material." Nikki stepped further away from the horse, reluctant to admit she was carting around illegal drugs. That would be another black mark in Hillman's book.

"But what specifically?" Colleen asked. "Any chance it's toilet paper? Or doggy doo bags? Because lately Sugar's trying to head toward a certain shit shack."

Nikki tilted her head. "Which one?"

"A portable by the back fence, near the gap where we take our horses for a break. Stupid place for a shitter. Some asshole actually yelled at me for letting Sugar walk too close."

"Do you know Cedro Rugger? Was he the guy who yelled?"

"Don't know the name other than when you asked about him earlier. But he strutted around like he was God's gift. I gave him the finger for being an asshole."

Nikki laughed. Colleen's bluntness was always refreshing. However, she quickly sobered. Because a portable in an odd place was worth checking out, especially if Cedro was involved.

CHAPTER TWENTY-NINE

It took a while for Nikki to find the porta potty. It sat alone, almost unnoticeable, against a mesh fence and inconveniently located for foot traffic. As Colleen noted, it probably didn't get much use.

There was no company name on the side or a contact number. A red occupied sign was displayed above the handle but when she pulled on the door, it swung open. The interior was very clean although the dispenser lacked toilet paper. There was no odor either, at least according to her nose.

She glanced over her shoulder, checking Gunner's reaction. But he was more intent on sniffing around the outer base where dandelions and tall grass flourished. That would also explain Sugar's interest.

That notion was blown when Gunner lifted his head and growled, staring in the direction of the barns. The only person there who consistently caused him to have that reaction was Cedro. The man might hope quitting his job would prevent questions about Ricky but Gunner's reaction showed Cedro's scent was fresh. It should be easy to follow, as long as he hadn't driven off in his car.

Her phone app confirmed his vehicle was still parked in the same spot so she gave Gunner the command to find.

He tugged her toward the barns, following a different route than she'd ever taken: a shortcut that crisscrossed between shedrows, picnic tables and around yellow flower beds. She let him run at speed, doing her best to keep up.

They rounded a frayed hammock then ducked beneath a flapping clothesline strung behind a workers' dorm. Gunner paused by the side door, but only for a moment. Then he shot past the building, emerging at the rear of a shedrow.

Three sweaty Thoroughbreds circled on a mechanical hot walker, less than twenty feet away. The horses jerked in surprise at their sudden appearance and a blaze-faced chestnut reared. A groom hurried over, scowling his disapproval.

Nikki gave a breathless apology and slowed Gunner to a more sedate jog. She'd be annoyed too if someone raced past their barn, scaring horses. And she didn't need any more complaints filed with security.

Still, if she could find Cedro, a slap on the wrist would be worth it. The police would want to talk to him but they had to find him first. And she'd love to help with that. Gunner was doing his part. He seemed to be heading toward the kitchen, following the shortest route. Cedro obviously knew all the short cuts.

A mustached man in a cowboy hat called a greeting, and she threw him a quick wave, saving her breath. It was hard keeping up with a powerful dog and no handler wanted to be a dead weight. She and Justin spent a lot of time in their home gym, but now she resolved to spend even more.

She smelled frying food before the kitchen was visible, confirming that Cedro had headed straight for Andrea. Had she known he was coming and that's why she'd been so scared? Their relationship seemed volatile but at least he couldn't hurt her in a public place. Horse people were tough, and few would stand idle if someone was threatened.

But Cedro had never reached the kitchen. Gunner stopped thirty feet before the building then circled on the road, whining with frustration.

Dammit. Someone must have picked him up, perhaps driven him back to his car. She checked her app, surprised to see Cedro's Toyota was still parked in the same spot. She gave Gunner a pat, sharing his disappointment. They both hated losing a trail because of a vehicle. It felt like cheating. At least she had the tracker on his car. He'd pick it up sometime and of course she'd send his location to Justin, who could pass it on to Detective Wilson. Obviously the detective would be much more receptive to information supplied by Justin.

Nikki's phone pinged, announcing a text. Andrea's message arrived five minutes before the arbitrary one-hour deadline: *Meet you behind the maintenance building, the one close to staff parking lot.*

Nikki grimaced. There'd be no trouble finding that spot. She'd stood outside the same building last night, listening to their grunts and whispers. It was a stark reminder the woman might be involved in whatever sketchy enterprise Pope was running, every bit as much as Cedro.

Andrea might be frightened. That didn't mean she was innocent.

CHAPTER THIRTY

I t only took a few minutes for Nikki to arrive at the meeting spot. The padlock on the maintenance building was locked, and the area appeared deserted. A bucket rattled and reggae music sounded from a nearby shedrow. Still, this had to be one of the most private spots on the backside.

Clearly Andrea didn't want to be seen with Nikki. Or she had another reason to pick this place.

Nikki checked for possible hiding spots then rounded the cinderblock building, confident Gunner would alert her to any trap. And right now his tail was wagging, a sure sign that Andrea had come alone.

Andrea had been facing the other way but she wheeled at their approach, holding her hands up, as if in supplication.

"Ricky's fine!" she said, talking fast. "So I don't need your help anymore. I just wanted to say thank you. So now you can go back to your paying work."

"That's great news," Nikki said. "I'm looking forward to meeting him. How about after school today?"

Andrea shook her head. "No, you can't! He's off visiting his dad. He'll be with him, you know, for a while. He hasn't seen much of him. That's why Ricky took off on his bike."

Andrea was a poor liar. Her gaze darted to the left, then to her feet, looking everywhere but at Nikki's face. And her words came in a rush, as if delivering them from memory.

Nikki waited, letting the silence grow uncomfortably long, guessing the woman would be the first to fill it. The more Andrea revealed, the easier it would be to figure out what was really going on.

"So please don't come to the kitchen again," Andrea said.

Bingo, Nikki thought. "You don't want Cedro to see us together?"

"No, yes." Andrea crossed her arms, her voice almost pleading. "Just stay away. Please. It's best for Ricky."

There was no doubt the woman seemed genuinely worried about her son.

"Help me understand," Nikki said, her voice softening. "Why is it better if I stay away? I know you were with Cedro last night, even though you told me the relationship was over."

A flush climbed Andrea's neck. "Cedro's going to bring Ricky back. He promised. But he can't be seen with me."

"So he's afraid of someone at the track? Who exactly?"

"I don't know. But he avoids the cameras, even more than usual. He texted around eight this morning, told me to get rid of you. And when he drove me home last night, he helped me write a note for Ricky."

"What did it say?"

"To wait at the apartment. To bring what he took from Pope, and Cedro would help make everything right. But Cedro was supposed to pick me up after my shift this morning and he didn't show. He isn't answering his phone either. So now I don't know what's going on. He must have decided to go to my apartment and wait for Ricky without me."

Nikki was already moving, figuring how many minutes it would take to race to her car.

"Why are you running?" Andrea called. "Are you going to my place? Can I get a drive?"

"Only if you can keep up." Nikki frantically checked her phone, comforted to see that Cedro's car hadn't moved. And already Andrea was running beside her, sticking to Nikki's side like a worried mother who didn't intend to be left behind.

"Is there more I should know?" Nikki asked. "Did Cedro say anything else last night?"

"He barely talked."

"I didn't hear him say much either," Nikki said.

Andrea scowled. "I was trying to please him. Thought sex might put him in a good mood and he'd tell me where Ricky is. But I don't think he knows. And he's mad at Ricky. Says he stole something from Pope, and now his boss is furious with all of them."

"Who's his boss?"

"Don't know." Andrea was panting now, her words running together. "Thought Cedro was Pope's boss but now I'm not sure. Cedro seems really worried."

"Did he say anything about Pope? Or his porta potty business?"

Andrea sped up, her hands fisting, as if hoping to escape more questions. But Nikki and Gunner easily kept pace.

"If I'm going to help," Nikki said, "you need to tell me everything. Unless you think Cedro will put Ricky's welfare over his sketchy business interests. And if Cedro is worried about being watched, it means someone higher than him is calling the shots. Someone who doesn't know Ricky."

And someone who doesn't care if he gets hurt, Nikki thought. But the body at Pope's property hadn't been identified yet. There was little to gain by sending Andrea into a panic. Not unless the woman needed more incentive.

They were both silent as they jogged toward Nikki's car, their breaths mingling in the air. Andrea was clearly exhausted, too winded to talk. But she had game, wasn't stopping. And when she stumbled, Nikki took pity on her.

"My car's close now," she said. "We can take a break while I check something."

The app showed a green dot still hovering over the far end of the track. Cedro hadn't moved his car and at this point, if he left for Andrea's house, they'd have a good chance of beating him there.

Andrea bent, clutching her stomach while Gunner studied the woman with worried brown eyes. Her dog had more empathy than her, Nikki thought. He was definitely the kinder soul.

"Let's walk the rest of the way," she said. "While you think about how much you trust Cedro."

"Not so much now," Andrea muttered, still holding her stomach. "He promised to pick me up this morning. Told me we'd wait for Ricky together. But he didn't show. Didn't even call."

"Did you know he quit his job this morning?"

"What? That's weird."

Nikki made an encouraging sound but Andrea just shook her head, still struggling to catch her breath.

"Weird?" Nikki prompted.

"Just yesterday he prepaid for another month of coffee," Andrea said. "Why would he waste money if he planned to quit?"

A lot of people would panic if they found a dead body. Which made it more likely Cedro hadn't been involved in the murder. He was reacting as if the flattened bungalow door had been a shock. Maybe he wasn't trying to avoid questions. Maybe he was just running.

But who was he afraid of and why was he still hanging around the track, if not to see Andrea? And what were his intentions with Ricky: hand him over to the killer or help the boy?

"What do you suppose Ricky stole?" Nikki kept her tone conversational, knowing anything more might put Andrea on the defensive.

"Ricky isn't a thief," Andrea said hotly. "He got in some trouble before but never for stealing."

"He took something that several people want," Nikki said. "It had to be something small, that he could carry on his bike. I'm guessing drugs."

"But Ricky doesn't do drugs. Your dog didn't smell anything in his room."

"Likely he was caught up by accident. Did Cedro ever say anything that made you think they were distributing drugs through the porta potty business?"

Andrea shook her head but her expression showed a growing horror. "Ricky wanted a new bike. So I encouraged him to take the job. Cedro made it sound like he was doing us a favor."

Ricky was young and Cedro knew he didn't talk much to his mom. They were barely home at the same time. Andrea had little support, and no trust in the police. Her son had been the perfect errand boy and the right age not to ask questions.

But this gang was ruthless in eliminating weak links. They'd demonstrated that with Pope. And according to Cedro's ex, Pope was high on the food chain. He must have made a significant mistake to be taken out. Of course, that was assuming the ravaged body was Pope.

"Let's just get to your apartment," Nikki said, urging Andrea back into a jog. And praying they'd be the first ones to arrive.

CHAPTER THIRTY-ONE

"Stop!" Andrea jerked forward in the passenger seat. "You drove past my apartment."

"Just checking the surroundings." Nikki kept her foot on the accelerator, maintaining a steady speed. Not too fast, not too slow. Nothing that would draw attention. "Do you see any unfamiliar cars? Anything look different?"

"No." Andrea reached for the door handle. "Drop me off. Ricky might be waiting."

Someone else might be waiting as well, Nikki thought, keeping the car moving. "I'm going to park in the back alley. Have Gunner check the area first. He'll let us know if anyone is inside."

"But Cedro isn't here. I don't see his car." Andrea's head swiveled, concern for her son outweighing any semblance of caution.

"Don't twist around," Nikki said. "Look without turning your head. And you need to give me your house key and wait in the car. Be ready to call 911."

"Is that necessary? Who do you think is inside?"

"Hopefully only Ricky." Nikki parked the car in the alley and shut off the ignition. Likely Cedro wasn't here. The tracker showed his Toyota was still on the backside.

However, she stuffed the Glock in the waistband of her jeans, careful to tug down her shirt and hide the bulge. Ricky had been running scared for days. A gun-wielding stranger could send him scooting back into hiding.

Andrea passed her a blue doll keychain with two keys, her wide eyes fixed on the gun. "How will I know if I should call for help?"

"If I'm not back in five minutes," Nikki said, motioning for Gunner to jump out.

Andrea cradled her phone, fingers posed over the screen. "I hope Ricky is in there. And nobody else."

Me too, Nikki thought, heading toward the rear of the apartment and keeping Gunner leashed. Blind searches were a bit of a crap shoot but she trusted him to sniff out any danger. He would certainly react to Ricky's scent. Although Ricky wasn't the one who had her worried.

Gunner trotted across the dry grass, pausing to check out a candy wrapper. Then he moved on, drawn to the dirt below the back window. He rose on his hind legs then dismissed it and circled to the front door where he sniffed at the steps.

He reacted as she'd hoped: a relaxed snuffle by the door knob along with a tail wag. Clearly the last person to enter this way had been Andrea.

Nikki tried both keys. The first one didn't fit but the second slid in smoothly. She pushed open the door and followed Gunner inside. The place felt benign. Everything appeared neat and tidy. No more vandalism.

The only items on the pristine counter were a loaf of bread and a lined sheet of paper, anchored by the doctored jar of peanut butter. Nikki scanned the note. A short but heartfelt message: a mother's plea for her son to wait here until she returned from work.

If it had been written under duress, it was impossible to tell. Of course, last night Andrea had thought Cedro was firmly on her side.

Obviously Ricky hadn't been here to see the note. Even if he'd chosen not to wait, he would have grabbed the food. He was smart not to return, knowing dangerous people were looking for him, and he was proving very adept at hiding. Possibly he'd ridden his bike deeper into the mountains.

Nikki moved down the hall and checked his bedroom. All his clothes had been picked up and the room straightened. Gunner gave some cursory sniffs but was more interested in stalking a bug that was flying erratic circles against the glass. Andrea had taken her advice and locked the window but it was understandable why it had been routinely left open. The room was sweltering.

The door slammed and eager steps sounded in the hall.

"Ricky?" Andrea peered in the bedroom, her shoulders slumping as she absorbed the empty room. "I waited almost five minutes. When Gunner didn't bark, I thought it was probably safe."

She didn't understand the magnitude of the danger. But whoever was looking for Ricky seemed to know he wasn't coming home. Maybe he was staying away to protect his mom.

Catching a nimble kid on a bike was a challenge, but the police would likely mount an extensive search once they confirmed Pope's identity and likely criminal involvement. But it would be a breakneck race to find Ricky before his pursuers did.

And unfortunately the killers had a head start.

CHAPTER THIRTY-TWO

Nikki's phone buzzed. Justin's name showed on the display and she stepped out of Ricky's bedroom to take the call.

"I just had a call from Detective Wilson," Justin said with a chuckle. "I gather you two had a little run-in this morning."

Nikki pressed the phone tighter to her ear, signaling to Andrea that she was going outside. She closed the front door and sat on the bottom step, Gunner by her side.

"She was too disinterested to have a run-in," Nikki said. "Did she complain about something?"

"No, only checking your creds. Just good police work. "

"Good police work would mean pushing for a search for Ricky. She wasn't very receptive."

"She's actually the detective who signed out your drug sample. She was in the area so they sent her out, thinking an unfortunate hiking accident would be a quick wrap."

"That explains her reluctance to consider it suspicious."

"I'm sure you set her straight." The amusement disappeared from Justin's voice. "When were you going to tell me about the body? Sounds like this is getting serious."

Nikki shifted back, feeling the edge of the concrete press into her spine. Finding a missing person was always serious and sadly it sometimes involved foul play. She suspected Justin would prefer she concentrate on white collar crime, or official police searches where there was professional backup. His worry was understandable, considering the murderers he routinely faced and the evil he knew was out there.

However, no one could have a better partner than Gunner. He sat beside her now, ever alert, never questioning her decisions or why she took on so many pro bono cases. He threw all his energy into helping the vulnerable, every bit as much as she did.

"Where are you now?" Justin's voice sharpened. "At the kid's house? Do you think the mother's in danger?"

Nikki gave a rueful smile. Justin's instincts were as well honed as Gunner's. "Yes, I'm at her apartment. I think she's part of the reason Ricky is staying away. He wants to protect his mom."

"So you think he's still alive?"

"Of course!" She spoke so emphatically, Gunner rose, looking for whatever had bothered her. "They're trying to lure him in," she added more quietly. "Just last night Cedro persuaded her to leave a note, telling him to wait at home."

"And he didn't wait. So now you're in limbo."

"Ricky didn't come back to see the note. I believe he's hiding somewhere in the wilderness park, but he's on a bike and very nimble. And I'm not sure how much of a search the police will do. A lot depends on the identity of the body, and how they decide to proceed." She gave a loaded pause, hoping for enlightenment.

"Just a sec." Steps sounded. Justin's office door clicked shut and the background noise disappeared.

"I expect," he said, "that Wilson will prioritize the search. Close the park and bring in a helicopter, maybe by three o'clock this afternoon. Especially if the victim was discovered to be Jeremiah Pope, an active drug dealer known to the task force."

"So it was Pope!" Nikki rose to her feet, elated. "Ricky was smart to run."

"Very smart." Justin's voice turned grim. "Pope is linked to the fentanyl deaths. But he's not the head of the snake. Early estimate is that he's been dead for days."

Nikki scanned the quiet street, the back of her neck tingling. So someone higher in the drug ring was chasing Ricky. Someone who Cedro considered more dangerous than Pope. How long could Ricky stay ahead of them?

She rose from the step, her voice lifting with urgency. "I have to go back there. Need to retrace Pope's steps. Gunner might pick up something."

"Impossible. The place is sealed off. I might be able to get you in under a search and rescue op, but that would take time."

"Ricky doesn't have time. Apparently he took something from them, likely drugs. So his mother's safety is a concern. Whoever's chasing him could show up here. Use her as leverage to bring in Ricky."

"I'll ask Wilson to post a security detail," Justin said, his voice smooth and calming. "In addition to searching for Ricky, she's prioritized finding Cedro Rugger. Said you gave her the man's name. I recall he's the track employee who threatened our horses?"

"Yes, but he quit his job this morning. He has to be tied to all this." She filled Justin in on Andrea's relationship with Cedro and how he'd found Ricky the porta potty job. Detective Wilson would give more credence to information coming from Justin.

It was comforting that the police and their vast resources were taking over the case. But she couldn't help worrying about Ricky, wondering what he was eating, how he was staying warm. By now, he must be too frightened to think.

"I'll also give Travis Hillman a call," Justin said. "Request a BOLO on Cedro and extra security around the kitchen. With his team, Ricky's mother will be safe at work as well as at home."

"Thank you, detective," Nikki said, pushing away her ambivalence. The cavalry had arrived. Andrea would be protected and police would find Ricky. Now she could focus on other things. Maybe drive out to Sonja's, see if her friend wanted another sweep of her house.

But the prospect didn't fill her with much excitement. Helping a vulnerable kid was far more rewarding. And judging by Gunner's solemn expression, he felt the same way.

CHAPTER THIRTY-THREE

"Yes," the park ranger told Nikki, his voice crisp and officious over the phone. "We have had several reports of food theft. Definitely higher than usual. Haven't seen a kid camping illegally though. Are you with the police?"

"Working with them," she said, thanking the ranger and ending the call before he could ask any more questions. Detective Wilson wouldn't appreciate her involvement. But it was reassuring Ricky was successfully scrounging food, doing whatever it took to survive. Good for him. Now she could stop worrying about him, at least until Justin's next update.

She turned her car into Sonja's driveway and rattled over the Texas gate. Several cackling chickens flapped their wings, irritated by the disturbance. But no other animals were loose and there didn't seem to be any new rescues. All the back paddocks were empty. Obviously Sonja's attention was still focused on her brother.

Nikki parked in front of the house and stepped out to a man's friendly holler.

"Hey, Nikki," Liam called. "Good to see you again!"

She felt a spike of guilt. His welcome wouldn't be so warm if he knew the reason she was here.

"Missed you the other day," Liam added, walking up to the car and peering into the back. "Gunner looks thirsty. I just filled the water trough. He can jump in and cool off if he'd like."

Nikki gave a grateful smile, letting Gunner out and motioning that he was free to roam. Like his sister, Liam was an animal lover and kind to the core. He'd helped build several of the original corrals back when Sonja was starting her rescue ranch.

He looked okay considering his recent brush with death, although his face was noticeably gaunt. A belt held up his jeans, and an oil-stained rag hung from his back pocket. He seemed prepared for work, not hiking. Sonja's worry about his frequent disappearances into the mountains didn't seem to be an issue today.

"Sonja's inside." Liam's smile slid from his face. "Bet she's watching from the window though, stressing when I'm out of sight. She thinks I'll find drugs behind every tree. And that sucks because I enjoy hiking."

Nikki silently empathized. The San Gabriel Wilderness may have been dangerous years ago but it was no longer the preferred hiding place for criminals. And in her mind, hiking could be an important part of rehab.

"Living out here is a big switch from the city," she said, trying to be diplomatic. "How are you making out?"

"I begged her to help. Know I should be grateful." He rubbed the back of his neck. "Getting out in nature helps, and it's not like I'm looking for a fix. Not really. But fighting this isn't easy. I'm wrecking her life too."

Nikki reached out and wrapped him in a hug. She wasn't usually a touchy-feely person but hearing his honesty, understanding what Sonja was dealing with, left her aching for them both. Sometimes a hug went far deeper than words.

"Thanks for bringing our groceries so she doesn't agonize about leaving me," Liam murmured before lowering his arms. His face brightened. "The past couple weeks it's been easier to stay busy. I'm fixing bikes and all the parts can be ordered online. Later, I'll move on to car repair."

That made sense. Liam had trained as a mechanic. Last year, he'd fixed her ignition problem, even when he'd been so high he could barely find the hood release. That was when she realized Sonja's brother had a drug problem. The fact that he was working with his hands again was a positive step.

"I'll be your first customer," she said. "My car will need new shocks, tires too. Some of the places I drive are rough on rubber."

Liam gave a knowing nod. "You should see the shred job on a bike I pulled from the mountain. The entire bike was mangled."

"Can you fix it?"

"No, hauled it out because it's litter. Leave no trace, you know. But I did find two that are fixable. One is a real nice mountain bike. The other is electric. Guess the battery ran out of juice and the owner didn't want to push it out. Or maybe the terrain was more extreme than expected. Some people have more money than sense. They don't think to pack an extra battery or tool kit."

And not everyone was as handy as Liam, Nikki thought. Even if they had access to tools, they might be stumped about repairs.

"Maybe you're in the market for an e-bike?" Liam gestured toward the barn, his face lighting up. "Come, take a look. I'll sell it cheap. You won't find a better price."

His sudden enthusiasm reminded her of an over-eager beach vendor and she had to shake off the suspicion that he was trying to raise drug money. It must be hard on Sonja, questioning his every behavior. Tough on Liam too.

She followed him into the nearby barn, interested in spite of her concern. An e-bike wouldn't fit in her life but one of the Tanner boys might like it. She'd check with Sonja first though, before any cash landed in Liam's pockets.

It was refreshingly cool inside the red planked barn. Liam had set up a work station at the rear, next to Sonja's tractor. The e-bike had a place of honor, positioned on a sturdy wooden table beside a row of tools. The fender was twisted and it had several deep scratches but otherwise it looked surprisingly good.

"You're sure the owner isn't coming back for this?" she asked.

Liam grinned and picked up a signed piece of paper. *Free to any sucker who wants to push this dead weight out of here.*

Nikki laughed, running her hand over the solid frame. "What a find. I'm surprised Sonja isn't interested."

"She wants a traditional bike." Liam gestured at a black mountain bike with wide tires that looked tough enough to handle any terrain. "Like this beauty. I stayed up last night fixing her up. The green one over there will be Sonja's. Just waiting on a couple parts."

The black mountain bike was indeed a beauty. Nikki even recognized the prestigious brand. No doubt it would bring a healthy chunk of change, far more than the e-bike.

She circled behind the table, admiring his collection of projects including a restored wheelbarrow and Sonja's future lime green bike. But it was the mangled bike lying in the corner that made her jerk to a standstill. For a moment, she even quit breathing.

Then she rushed forward, propped the bike against the wall, and pulled out her phone.

"Don't bother looking at that one," Liam said. "It's going to the dump. Not much of a bike to start with."

She barely heard him, concentrating instead on pulling up the picture of Ricky's bike. It was hard to compare the original with this twisted version, but the size seemed the same. So did the color. But she needed an expert's advice.

"Help me, Liam," she called over her shoulder. "Is this the same bike as the one on my phone?"

Liam stepped closer, his eyes sliding from the picture to the bike. "Possibly," he said. "They both have a school safe sticker on the seat post."

She peered closer, trying to see what he'd noticed. The sticker was hard to make out, but once she bent and wiped the dust off, it was clearly visible. "Where and when did you find this?"

"Yesterday," he said slowly. "On the northwest trail."

That was nowhere near Pope's bungalow but it explained why Ricky hadn't returned to his house. It would be a long way to go without a bike. Especially if he was injured.

"I'm looking for the boy who owns this bike," she said. "Did you see him around? Possibly hurt in the fall?"

Liam jerked back as if insulted. "No way. And I would never leave an injured kid in the mountains."

"Of course not. But he's running from some dangerous men and he's very scared. He may have hidden."

"What's he mixed up with?" Liam abruptly turned his back and grabbed a wrench, tossing it expertly in his hand.

"Drug dealers." She edged sideways so she could see his expression but his face showed nothing but concern. Perhaps she'd misinterpreted his sudden evasiveness.

"Probably not the same kid," he said. Still gripping the wrench, he turned to the bike and gave it a more thorough inspection. "Those stickers are all over the schools. And now that I look closer, the handlebars are different. A drop bar, not a bullhorn."

She checked the picture then the bike. The handlebars looked the same to her but it was impossible to gauge the original shape, not the way these ones were twisted.

"I don't see how you can tell," she said.

"That's because you're not a mechanic." The edge in his voice showed he didn't want to talk about it anymore.

"Everything else looks identical though," she persisted. "Even the scrapes and torn seat."

"Are you questioning me?"

"Yes, I suppose I am."

"Don't. You can trust me."

Words that are often spoken by a liar. And she had a K9 partner that she trusted much more than Liam. She moved toward the doorway. Gunner was in the pony enclosure, his tail wagging as he played some sort of game with Stormy.

At her whistle, he leaped over the railing, loped into the barn and stared up at her expectantly.

"Find," she said, ignoring Liam's dramatic eye roll.

Gunner trotted a half circle then bee lined toward the mangled bike. He sat beside it, tail thumping on the planked floor, sending dust motes swirling in the air. She hadn't expected him to be so fast. Wasn't sure if the bike would be enough but obviously the torn seat held Ricky's scent.

"Good dog." She patted Gunner, her gaze pinned on Liam. "I need to know the exact spot where you found this bike."

"Hard to remember," he said.

"Try." She pulled up a map of the wilderness park and held her phone screen in front of him.

"Are you interested in a bike?" Sonja called, her cheery voice coming from the doorway. "You'll have to get in line. I'm waiting on the pretty green one but who knows what he'll find next week."

She walked closer, her steps faltering as she absorbed the tension. "What's wrong? Gunner found drugs, didn't he? I knew he would!"

"Not drugs," Nikki said quickly, shooting her a reassuring smile. "But Gunner reacted to one of the bikes Liam found. I believe it belongs to the missing boy."

"Oh, Liam," Sonja wailed. "What are you mixed up with? Is that why you had my phone this morning? You were arranging a drug deal?"

"You're so damn quick to think I'm looking for a fix." Liam slammed the wrench on the table, the force sending a container of nails scattering over the floor. He stomped toward the door, fists so tight the tendons in his thin arms bulged.

He jerked to a stop, only briefly and only to yell. "I'm sick of the way you're always watching! Well, screw you. And screw the bikes!"

CHAPTER THIRTY-FOUR

The barn turned quiet following Liam's outburst. Even Gunner looked surprised, his head cocked toward the empty doorway.

Sonja dropped onto the bench, groaning. "Sorry about that. His mood swings are painful. Probably he should check into rehab, if only for the sake of our relationship."

"If it's financing, I can help."

"I have the money." Sonja gave Nikki a wobbly smile. "But we both thought he'd be happier here. The past couple of weeks have been fairly smooth. He seemed genuinely enthused about the bike gig."

"I thought he was too," Nikki said. "He only got upset when I asked where he'd found the bike."

"You really think it belongs to your missing kid?"

"Positive, judging by the way Gunner reacted."

Sonja shoved a tendril of hair behind her ear then pulled it out again. "Give him a few hours to calm down. Then we can ask him together. I'm sure he'll want to help. He's always been a kind person."

Maybe. But Nikki realized she hadn't been imagining Liam's evasiveness. His sudden huff might have been the easiest way to walk away and avoid questions. She didn't want to sit on the verandah, twiddling her thumbs, while Ricky was out there alone. Possibly hurt, judging by the shape of his bike.

If he really was in this area, the official search teams would never find him. They'd closed one of the wilderness parks, but not the larger one adjoining Sonja's property. Gunner might be able to pick up his trail now that Ricky wasn't on a bike. But it was essential to narrow down a starting point.

And maybe that could be done. She swung toward Sonja, taut with hope. "Did you sew the tracker in Liam's backpack yet?"

"Yes." Sonja's eyes narrowed. "But I thought you weren't a fan of that. Suddenly your ethics have changed?"

"A boy is missing, Sonja."

"All right." Sonja heaved a reluctant sigh. "But I don't want *him* to know."

Nikki nodded and they moved to the doorway, peering outside. Stormy's ears were pricked, the pony's attention focused on something by the llama pen. Liam was behind the gate, throwing manure into a wheelbarrow, his arms jerky with emotion.

"Ok, he's too far away to hear." Sonja pulled out her phone, pressed the screen and passed it to Nikki. "Do you really think he met up with that kid?"

"Not sure," Nikki said, scanning Liam's routes even as she forwarded the information to her phone. "He said he found it yesterday on the northwest trail. So I'm going to head that way. See if Gunner can pick up a scent."

"But Liam found that bike two days ago. I remember he called it junk but that he was doing his part for the environment. And then he started working non-stop on the black mountain bike. He hasn't gone hiking since."

Nikki checked the dates. There was no activity yesterday. But two days ago, Liam had headed in an entirely different direction. One that ended along a steep cliff, close to a waterfall. It looked like a challenging trail even for the most advanced biker. But if someone wanted to stay hidden...

"You think it was Tuesday?" Nikki rocked back on her heels. Following the wrong route would be a huge time waste. But Liam had hesitated when she'd asked the day. He might have been lying when he claimed to have found it yesterday although there seemed no reason to not tell the truth.

"Tuesday, yes." Sonja nodded but her voice was distant, as if thinking of something else.

"Do you see something? Something about the trail?" Nikki didn't understand Sonja's psychic gift but she'd learned not to ignore it.

"Nope." Sonja blew the word out in frustration. "I'm empty. Stuck on seeing drugs behind every tree. No wonder Liam says I'm obsessed. But Wednesday he didn't hike and Monday was when he brought home the e-bike. He couldn't have pushed both. So it had to be Tuesday."

"Then Gunner and I will head toward the waterfall."

"If you wait for Liam to calm down, he could go with you. Then he can show you the exact spot."

"That's okay," Nikki said, already pressing out a text. She didn't want to enter the mountains with someone she didn't trust. And for extra security, she included her route in her message to Justin.

"I want to move fast on this," she said, softening her voice. "If I find something then the police can adjust their search co-ordinates. They'll want to talk to Liam as well."

"But he didn't do anything wrong. All he does is look for bikes to fix. He wouldn't leave anyone injured." Sonja fiddled with her hair again, her nervousness betraying her concern. "Besides, I would have sensed something. And all I'm feeling now is that it's important to keep him on the property. He's not knocking people down, stealing bikes, so he can score drugs."

Nikki blinked, surprised her friend had verbalized that fear. Nikki didn't think that either, not really. But Liam's evasiveness left her wary.

"I just want to bring Ricky home," Nikki said. "And the fact that Liam found his bike is helpful. He must have been really scared to leave a familiar area."

"I warned Liam," Sonja said. "Told him those mountains weren't safe. But he thinks my visions are hokey."

"And I don't. So if I haven't returned by sunset, let Justin know. Doubt I'll have cell coverage for long."

Sonja abruptly clutched Nikki's hand, her grip so tight that it hurt. "Be careful," she warned.

CHAPTER THIRTY-FIVE

The first part of the trail was relatively easy, a slow incline over packed dirt intermingled with granite slabs. The afternoon sun was hot but soothing on Nikki's shoulders. Hiking was one of her favorite pastimes and she stopped worrying about Ricky. She simply let her mind and body drift into a state of tranquility.

Gunner stayed twenty feet ahead, moving easily and enjoying the freedom. The terrain would change once the real climb started. Paw protection might be needed, depending on the rocks. For now though, his rubber booties could stay in her pack.

An hour later, Gunner jerked to a stop and her serenity vanished in a flash. She rose on the balls of her feet, searching for whatever left his tail stiff with warning. It didn't take long to spot the danger: A fat rattlesnake curled on a rock, only six feet away, as motionless as Gunner.

"It's okay," she said, motioning him forward. She lengthened her stride, taking a wide berth around the rock. Gunner knew not to mess with snakes but his warning was appreciated. It was a good reminder that this wasn't a Sunday walk in the park.

The trail narrowed, twisting upwards in a series of switchbacks, the climbing made more difficult by a resistant wind. She tried to keep a steady pace but her leg muscles protested, demanding a break.

She opened a bottle of water, poured some in Gunner's portable bowl and took an appreciative swig. Then she splurged and splashed the layer of grit from her face, deciding that anybody who chose this trail was searching for someone. Or running from something.

This section was a rocky wilderness, waiting to trip visitors up at the slightest misstep. And the critters that lived here were as inhospitable as the land. She checked the sky, trying not to think about hungry coyotes and how they'd ripped apart Pope's body. Thankfully the stark blue was empty of any circling vultures.

Maybe only Ricky's bike had been hurt. Not the rider. He'd probably chosen this area knowing his pursuers would never find him. It was a good choice if one didn't want to be found. Even so, it was almost inconceivable that a twelve-year-old would want to be alone in such desolate country, and she couldn't help but admire his courage.

She'd spent time as a teen runaway, but she'd holed up in city parks, surrounded by street lights and honking cars. She'd also had Justin checking on her, encouraging her to return home and finish school. Ricky had no one. And he was too far away to slip back to his mother's house for a shower and sandwich.

She continued climbing, with Gunner and her thoughts for company. They only stopped when a service road cut the hiking trail. Had Ricky taken that wider road? It would have been easier to bike. And there'd be more chance of running into some four wheelers, riders who could carry more supplies and might be amenable to sharing their food.

She hesitated. The only visible tracks were that of an off-road vehicle, but the swirling dust would have covered evidence of a bike. The four wheeler was recent, considering the gusty wind.

Gunner stuck his nose in the air. Then he swung east along the service road, moving with purpose. He seemed to be following an air scent rather than a trail so likely Ricky had still been on his bike at this point.

She followed, tired but encouraged. Then she noticed something peculiar: His hackles had risen.

She checked for gray shadows, wondering if he smelled coyotes. Their recent encounter was likely fresh in his brain and it was understandable he'd be distracted. But being sidetracked by wild animals wasn't good, especially when much of their search and rescue work involved remote country.

However, he was moving stiff-legged, not charging forward as he would after a coyote or a target scent. And his hair was up, from his hackles to his tail, leaving a clear warning line.

She shifted the pack to her chest, opened the top zipper and grabbed her pepper spray. No doubt, some of Gunner's wariness stemmed from the swirling wind and the difficulty in pinpointing a scent's origin. For now, she'd have to trust her dog. He clearly believed there was danger ahead. Maybe a bear?

And then the silence was broken. Not by a coyote yip or the angry huff of a black bear, but a human shout.

CHAPTER THIRTY-SIX

Nikki froze, straining to trace the voice's origin. It sounded like a man, possibly the one who'd driven the four wheeler. Maybe the shout was unrelated to Ricky but her instincts said otherwise. So did Gunner's growl.

"Quiet," she whispered, clipping on his leash and edging forward. The voice seemed to have come from the west, above the road and beyond a cluster of pines.

She eased through the trees and soon spotted the back of a parked vehicle. Not a four wheeler but a beefy utility vehicle, capable of carrying four adults. She crept closer, scanning the sides, hoping to see a park ranger decal. But other than the dust blurring the camouflage paint, the vehicle lacked any markings. There was no fishing rod or hunting gear. And no rifle.

She took several pictures, including the green OHV plate then backed into the shelter of the scrubby pines, not comforted by the lack of a firearm. It might mean the driver was carrying. Gunner remained quiet but his hackles were still up, another reason to remain unseen. At least for now.

Then a voice rang out again, a chillingly familiar voice. It was Cedro and there was no doubt that he was here for the same reason as she was. Especially when he yelled: "Ricky, get your ass down here."

That damn car tracker was her first thought. She'd been comforted believing Cedro was still at the track. But an accomplice must have picked him up outside the kitchen, driven him to a trailhead and provided him with an off-road vehicle.

The mystery was how he'd known where to find Ricky. Had Andrea lied again? But she didn't know Ricky's location. She'd genuinely expected to find him at her house this morning. Andrea certainly didn't know where Nikki had headed. Only Justin and Sonja knew that.

Skirting the sound of Cedro's voice, Nikki headed uphill, taking a circuitous route through the stunted trees and boulders, every muscle taut as she tried to stay hidden. But the loose rock was treacherous and pebbles shifted beneath Gunner's paws, rolling downhill with a clatter.

She stilled, hoping the wind would cover the noise. But Cedro shifted, his voice moving alarmingly close.

"I hear you, Ricky," he called. "Come on out. Everything will be okay. They just want you to return the drugs. Then I can drive you home to your mom."

Shit. Cedro thought she was Ricky. He was less than twenty feet away. And moving closer.

Gunner growled and she tapped his muzzle in warning, accepting they couldn't stay hidden much longer. The cliff was too steep for Gunner to climb, and too exposed. But if she could get a visual, at least she'd know if Cedro was armed.

She pressed against a granite boulder and slipped the Glock from her pack. At this point, she had the element of surprise. There hadn't been a rifle in the vehicle and it was doubtful Cedro would be carrying anything so visible while calling for Ricky to step out.

There was also the possibility he didn't intend to hurt the boy. Andrea seemed certain of that. However Nikki wasn't as convinced.

She inched sideways, peeking around the boulder and staying low to the ground. Cedro was staring at a spot to her left. His hands were in the air, palms open. If he were armed, it was only with a handgun, likely tucked in the back of his jeans.

Her heart kicked in relief and she adjusted her grip on the gun. Time to step out. Disarm the man. Find Ricky. She just needed to take some deep breaths, steady herself.

Below, a squirrel scolded. Then rocks rattled. She froze, realizing that Cedro wasn't alone. There were two of them. Things just got a lot more dicey.

"Okay," a boy's voice called from above. "I'm coming down."

"There you are," Cedro said, sounding surprised at Ricky's location as he moved away from Nikki. "Come on out. Bring the drugs."

"What about those men? The ones who killed Pope?"

"Shut up! You didn't see anything. Now get down here and we'll forget what happened."

"Are you mad at me?"

"Yes, I'm mad," Cedro said, the crunching sound growing fainter as he angled away from Nikki's hiding spot. "But I promised your mother I'd find you. Now throw me the package. That'll go a long way to getting you out of this mess."

"I didn't plan to take it. But Pope owed me money."

"Asswipe was skimming everywhere," Cedro said. "But you picked the wrong people to steal from. At least you had the sense to send me a message."

He sounded more resigned than angry. Ricky must have thought so too because a white plastic package sailed through the air, falling on the ground near Cedro's feet. Seconds later, a disheveled boy stepped out from behind a circle of boulders, only a stone's throw from Nikki.

"Hope you brought some food," Ricky said, a grin cutting his face. "I'm starving." He twisted to pick something up just as pieces of rock exploded around him.

"No!" Cedro yelled. But the rifle kept firing, the staccato of a semi-automatic raking the rocks.

Gunner barked. Nikki grabbed his muzzle, waiting for the flurry of bullets to stop. Finally it turned deathly quiet. Even the scolding squirrel was silent.

She waited for a long moment. Then belly crawled to the side of the boulder, checking over the top of her Glock, cautiously searching for the shooter. It hadn't been Cedro who'd fired. He was lying on his stomach, dark liquid oozing around his head. Likely gone.

So was the packet of drugs.

CHAPTER THIRTY-SEVEN

"Quiet," Nikki whispered, her heart pounding as she peered around the rock, trying to establish the killer's position. Gunner was trained to stay down during a shooting but he'd let out that one bark. Whoever had come for Ricky, and shot Cedro, now knew she was here. At least she had high ground.

She considered squeezing off a warning shot then decided against it. If the shooter didn't know she was armed, he might rush up to finish them off. But the slope was empty. No sign of Ricky, only the white-chipped boulder where the bullets had sprayed. He'd moved at the perfect time.

Edging back, she pulled out her phone, not surprised to see there was no coverage. Gunner lay beside her, trying to be quiet, but his throat vibrated, his ears pointing downhill. At least the killer wasn't circling around them, and she was filled with a primal mixture of fear and relief.

Long minutes later, an engine roared to life.

She stuck her head around the rock and watched as the utility vehicle roared away. One occupant, impossible to see his face. He rounded the bend and disappeared, belching dust and exhaust.

"Are you okay, Ricky?" she called, rising and hurrying around the rock. "I'm Nikki, a friend of your mom's. She asked me to find you."

Nikki glanced at Cedro spread-eagled on the ground. He'd been Andrea's friend too. It was obvious Ricky had trusted him. She should check if first aid was warranted, but right now her concern was for Ricky. She didn't think he'd been hit but no sound came from above and a bullet might have ricocheted.

She stuffed her gun back in her pack before heading uphill, not wanting to scare him anymore. Even if he wasn't injured, he was likely frozen with fear. He'd been on the run for almost a week, been shot at, and had just witnessed the cold-blooded shooting of a family friend.

"I'm a private investigator, Ricky," she said, slowly approaching the ring of rocks. "And Gunner is a trained police dog. We're here to help."

She peered around the bullet-scarred rock then rocked back in surprise. The ring of boulders had been a great hiding place. But it was empty. Only a backpack and tangled sleeping bag marked his presence.

Ricky didn't trust her. Not surprising. But it was remarkable he'd been able to slip away so quickly. Her heart was still pounding, her legs stiff with adrenaline. Yet fear hadn't slowed his movement, or thinking process.

She scanned the service road, listening for an engine, hoping the shooter wouldn't return. He might be looking for a spot with cell phone coverage so he could gather further orders. If so, she didn't have much time. Clearly they wanted Ricky dead. He'd been the shooter's original target, even after tossing down the drugs.

Cedro hadn't expected that. He'd seemed shocked that his accomplice was shooting at the boy. And she couldn't follow Ricky in good conscience without first seeing if Cedro was alive.

She half-slid, half-jogged down the hill but it was clear there'd be no need to check for vitals. The back of Cedro's skull had been blown off.

Gunner tilted his head, looking solemn. This was the first time his hackles hadn't risen when he was close to the man. However, he understood death and knew Cedro was no longer a threat.

He stuck close to her side as she hurried back to Ricky's last hiding spot. A shower of rocks clattered down the slope but noise wasn't a concern, at least for now. Even the squirrel judged it to be safe again, scolding their intrusion from a twisted pine branch.

She let Gunner sniff Ricky's sleeping bag. This had been a smartly chosen hiding spot with a smooth slab to sit on, protected by boulders, and a sweeping view of the fire road. There wasn't much room to move but it would have been comfortable for a wiry twelve-year-old.

Gunner lifted his head, whining with eagerness. Clearly he had the scent. And Ricky couldn't be far away.

"Find," she said.

CHAPTER THIRTY-EIGHT

Ricky's breath came in painful gasps and he stumbled to a stop, too exhausted to keep climbing. It was hard to believe that Cedro had been shot, blood and junk oozing from his head just like on a video game. And they were still chasing him. Worse, they'd brought a dog.

He was good at hiding but now he also had to cover up his smell. If only he had his bike.

One more day and that hiker, Liam, would have brought a replacement. At least that's what he'd said. But Ricky knew a drug addict when he saw one, and they were always spewing promises. Liam had turned euphoric when Ricky showed him the packet. Had promised him the moon, including food, a mountain bike, and also that he'd pass on a message to Cedro.

Clearly, Liam had fulfilled that last promise. Cedro had shown up at the right spot but it didn't appear he'd be leaving. Ricky wiped at his cheek, his hand coming away a slimy red. He gave an involuntary groan, picturing his head split like Cedro's. Then he realized it was only a cut, probably from the flying rock.

He dropped to his knees, weak with the knowledge they still wanted to kill him. He'd never see his mother again. She'd never know what had happened. She'd wait forever in that suffocating apartment, praying he'd return. Maybe she'd think he was somewhere safe with Cedro. But deep down, she'd know.

He drew in a shallow breath, trying to straighten his thoughts. To think. The wind had picked up but he could no longer hear any voices, or barking. On internet clips, the dogs always made a racket. This one was silent. Somehow that made it worse.

He could keep climbing but there was little cover and he didn't want to be picked off by that rifle. Probably best to follow the ledge and circle back to the waterfall. Dogs can't follow people through water, can they?

His chest hurt and his legs felt as if they belonged to someone else. But he wasn't going to curl up here and make it easy for them. Pushing himself to his feet, he continued picking his way along the side of the cliff, using the mountain peak to the west as a marker.

Finally he heard the crashing of the waterfall. He'd cross downstream, close to the rocky basin where he'd washed yesterday. The current was swift, blasting over a scatter of jagged rocks. Likely no person, or dog, would be desperate enough to follow. After all, they had the option of jumping in their all-terrain vehicle, finding a bridge and waiting on the other side.

He didn't want to think about what he'd do after he crossed the river. That damn dog changed everything. If he could evade it until he got the bike, he might have a chance, although he'd have to figure out another way to pay Liam. For now, he had bigger concerns.

He slid down a shale-cut slope, wincing at the rattle of rocks as he listened for barking. He could outrun most people, but not a dog, and he kept checking over his shoulder, wondering when it would be biting at his ass. A few more minutes though, and he'd be safe at the river.

Once he hit flat ground, he started running, straight toward the break in the trees that marked a game trail, the same spot where he'd met Liam. Hopefully he'd have time to catch his breath and study the river. The roughest water was near the middle but if he could keep a grip on the rocks, he should be able to stay on his feet.

Minutes later, he burst from the trees onto the riverbank. He skidded to a stop, swallowing in dismay. The river looked angrier today, with water roiling around pointed rocks, leaving frothy ridges of white along the shore. A band corded around his chest, the tightness not entirely from the long sprint. Now he had real misgivings about tackling that current.

He glanced behind him, checking the trail. Maybe no one was following and he wouldn't have to cross. The joke would be on them if they drove around to wait on the other side. Deep-down though, he knew they wouldn't give up. He'd thought returning the drugs would make it right. Cedro seemed to think so too. But they'd sucker shot him. And they knew Cedro; they didn't know him.

He rubbed his arms, feeling goose bumps along with his unfamiliar thinness. He wasn't in good shape to tackle a river and now he didn't even have his pack. No sleeping bag, jacket or even the tick repellant he'd scooped up from a campsite. Tomorrow he'd have to cross back again to meet Liam. Of course, that was only if he managed to evade the killers.

His knees weakened and he buckled, still staring at the menacing water. It felt as if he'd been running for months but this was the first time hiding wasn't an option. Fighting a dog, an ATV and an assault rifle seemed impossible. On the other hand, it was better to drown than curl up in a ball and be shot. It would suck to go out like a coward.

Lurching to his feet, he squared his shoulders and walked into the frigid river.

CHAPTER THIRTY-NINE

Gunner scrambled along the steep canyon wall, his tail waving like a flag. He was moving faster than Nikki but it was treacherous, and several times she warned him to slow. She didn't want either of them sliding to the rocks below. Ricky must be part mountain goat to have disappeared so fast.

It was understandable he'd run. He had no reason to trust her. Periodically, she stopped and identified herself, calling his name, but it was doubtful he even heard. The wind was too strong and he was nowhere in sight. With Gunner locked on his trail though, it was only a matter of time before she'd catch up.

Gunner suddenly shifted direction and scrambled down the slope. It was a steep spot for Ricky to have chosen to descend, but Gunner reached the bottom and was now loping across a section of flat land, headed toward a gap in some sycamore trees.

The air was thick with moisture, showing the waterfall was close. The river would be rough at its base. Hopefully Ricky wouldn't try to cross. At this elevation, any water was bound to be dangerous, with frigid temperatures, slippery rocks and powerful currents.

She also had to stay close to Gunner and keep him out of the river. There was no time for a cautious descent so she sat and slid, dislodging a shower of rocks and bouncing painfully over a jagged outcrop. Then she rose and sped after her dog.

A narrow game trail cut through the brush. She ducked numerous branches, stumbled over a protruding root, all the while calling for Gunner to slow. He either didn't hear or had elected to make his own decisions.

Ten minutes later, she burst from the shadows of the trees, her chest aching. The lowering sun highlighted a sparkling waterfall several hundred feet upstream, but she was too horrified to appreciate the view. The water in front of her was a frothing cauldron of fury. And Gunner stood in it, chest deep.

At first she couldn't figure out what he was watching. Then an arm moved and she spotted Ricky clinging to a submerged log as torrents of water sluiced over his shoulders.

He was almost mid-channel, too far out to reach. It was astonishing he'd made it that far. But the river curled further down where the current swept closer to the bank. She might have a chance to grab him there.

"Hang on, Ricky," she shouted, pulling off her pack and groping for her rope even as she scrambled downstream. There wasn't much time. He wouldn't be able to keep his grip for long. That log looked rotten, jammed between two rocks. Worse, he'd lost his footing, his legs thrashing on the surface of the water, vainly fighting the current.

She tied one end around a nearby tree then rushed into the shockingly-cold river, feeling for a foothold even as she looped the rope around her waist. Every inch of the twenty-foot length was precious but it took extra time to make a good knot, her fingers clumsy in the frigid water. Then she jammed her feet between two rocks and braced herself against the current.

Now she was ready. Ricky would have to help though.

"Aim toward me," she called, hoping he'd hear her over the roar. "Keep your feet pointed downstream."

For a second his gaze caught hers, the whites of his eyes matching the frothing river. Then the log shifted and he lost his grip. He yelped once, his cry cut off as he vanished below the surface. Seconds later, the river tossed him back up. But his feet were pointed upstream, his head pin-balling off the rocks.

She stretched, leaning as far as the rope would allow, realizing he wouldn't be able to steer her way. He was helpless, maybe unconscious. She'd have to hope he'd be close enough to grab.

Movement flashed. Damn. Gunner had torpedoed into the current, swimming downstream, his eyes locked on Ricky. She didn't want him in the river. It was no place for a dog. But when Ricky momentarily jammed between two rocks, Gunner was able to wrap his mouth around the boy's arm.

The only thing to do now was encourage him. "Good dog," she shouted. "Bring him!"

Time seemed to stand still as Gunner's shoulders churned, moving precious inches closer to the bank. And her. She winced as both he and Ricky hit a rock and were thrown sideways. At least they'd been pushed in the right direction.

There'd only be one chance to snag them, and even though she was poised and ready, she missed. Her reaching hands felt nothing but water...and Gunner's long tail.

She held on, relying on the rope to keep from being sucked in, straining to pull both Ricky and Gunner out of the current's fierce hold. Inch by inch, she edged back, arms feeling as if they were being pulled off. She felt a slight easing on the rope, then more. Finally the river gave up and she was able to tow them in to the sheltering bank.

Neither Ricky nor Gunner moved. They simply lay in the shallow water, Gunner's mouth still wrapped around Ricky's arm.

"It's okay," she said, trying to sound reassuring as she dragged them onto dry land. But Ricky's eyes were shut, his head bloody. She dropped to her knees, worry clogging her throat. However, a quick check showed his breathing and heartbeat were stable.

She moved to Gunner, running her hands over his ribs, relieved to find no obvious injury. His eyes were open but he was exhausted. He didn't always listen and sometimes made his own decisions, one of the reasons he hadn't flourished at K9 school. And while she never would have sent him into that river, he'd made the brave choice, and saved Ricky's life.

She swiped the water and tears from her face, praying neither of them was seriously hurt. But Ricky's head had slammed against the rocks and once he'd lost consciousness he'd been unable to protect himself. Gunner had been lucky and smart, largely able to avoid the rocks.

The most immediate concern was to warm them up. She'd have to risk making a fire and hope Cedro's killer didn't return. By now, Sonja would have called Justin, and that call, along with Nikki's earlier message, would prompt action. Justin would doubtlessly contact Detective Wilson and insist she check this location.

Still, that would take time. Police would need to organize off-road vehicles and move them to the closest trailhead. It would be dark soon and the terrain challenging, so help wouldn't arrive until tomorrow.

The urge to drag Ricky into the woods and hide him in the brush was overwhelming. Then she could set up a defensive position where she'd have a fighting chance of holding off a high-powered rifle.

Clearly, though, he shouldn't be moved. And it was critical to get him out of his wet clothes. Her own body was shaking with cold. Ricky's experience had been much worse and he'd been in the water longer.

She rummaged through her pack for matches and fire starter then gathered some twigs and branches. Had just lit the fire when a cold nose touched her neck.

"Hey, buddy," she said, delighted to see Gunner on his feet and wagging his tail. Not only was his company reassuring, but he could be relied on to warn of danger. Right now, he looked unconcerned, wandering over to sniff Ricky's face and then lying on the ground beside the boy.

It was then she noticed Ricky's twitch. And how his eyelids were clamped suspiciously tight.

"Can you hear me, Ricky?" she said. "I'm Nikki, a private investigator. My dog's name is Gunner."

She watched his face. Deathly pale but a muscle moved in his cheek. The rascal was only pretending to be unconscious.

"Your mom asked me to find you," she went on. "I have protein bars in my pack. Peanut butter ones. She said they were your favorite."

Ricky's eyes flickered open. He peered at his bare arm then turned his head toward Gunner, more puzzled than wary. "That dog grabbed me. Towed me in the water. But his teeth didn't even break my skin."

"He's a good boy," Nikki said. "Knows his own strength."

"So he won't bite?"

"He won't bite *you*," Nikki said.

"I don't like dogs. But I guess he's okay." Wincing, Ricky pushed himself to a sitting position. "I thought you came with the side-by-side. That you were the one who shot Cedro. So you know my mom?"

"Yes, we met at the track kitchen. She told me all about you. She's very worried."

"What about Cedro? Is he really dead?"

At her solemn nod, Ricky's mouth wobbled. He quickly averted his head, hiding his reaction. Turning, she scooped up some more branches. He clearly didn't like to show his emotions, and she just wanted him to feel comfortable.

"I'm going to build up the fire," she said, pulling a heat sheet from her pack and unfolding the shiny square. "Then we can get you out of your clothes, warm you up. Can you tell me where you hurt?"

He didn't answer. Was focused on studying the trees, as if anticipating trouble and mapping a getaway. His awareness had stood him in good stead, and she wondered if he expected the killer to follow. His next words confirmed it.

"The fire is nice and all," he said. "But I hope you brought a gun."

CHAPTER FORTY

"No one is close." Nikki shot Ricky a reassuring smile. "And it will take time to drive around to the nearest bridge." Unless the killer had been told to ditch his vehicle and follow them on foot. However, she didn't voice that possibility.

"But do you have a gun?" Ricky's teeth chattered, his skin so pale it was almost translucent, and his gaze kept shooting toward the trees. Clearly in flight mode.

"Yes, it's in my pack. And Gunner will give us plenty of warning. Let's get you out of those clothes so you can warm up." Ricky still looked dubious so she added: "Then if you need to, you'll be better able to run."

He nodded as if that made sense but didn't move. She knelt down and eased off his t-shirt, relieved that his arms moved normally. He had too many bruises to count but no huge gashes. There might be some cracked ribs but he didn't seem to feel pain. That would come later. His head injury was the biggest concern, but the cut didn't look deep and it had stopped oozing blood.

"Do you know what day it is?" she asked, tucking the heat sheet around his shoulders.

"Thursday. And I'm all right. Don't waste your time asking stupid questions."

Nikki grinned. This kid was a firecracker. "Then can you tell me how Cedro knew where you were hiding? And why they're chasing you?"

He gave her an appraising look as if considering his answer. "I wasn't thinking," he finally said. "Was mad I hadn't been paid so I grabbed the drugs. When they killed Pope, I ran. And I asked a hiker to call Cedro and tell him where I was."

Her fingers jerked and she almost dropped his shirt. This was bad. She hid her dismay by laying it by the fire and fiddling with its placement. "Do you remember the hiker's name?"

"Liam. He promised me a mountain bike in exchange for a bit of the coke."

Nikki squeezed her eyes shut. No wonder Liam had turned evasive.

"That's not going to happen now," Ricky went on. "I'll probably never be able to go home."

"Sure you will. The police want to stop this drug ring."

"I'm not talking to any cops." He tugged the heat sheet tighter around his shoulders, stubbornness strengthening his voice. "Then they'll really want to kill me. They didn't think twice about offing Cedro."

Nikki removed his sneakers then tugged off his drenched socks. Ricky paid little attention, only kept muttering that he was no damn snitch. And that he hadn't known about the drugs until his fateful bike ride.

Obviously he had nothing to lose by working with the detectives but he was almost in a fugue state, and she was just relieved he was no longer fixated on running. He'd shifted, leaning into Gunner's warm chest, talking more to himself than her.

But when he started grumbling about "stinking portables," she couldn't hold her curiosity.

"So drugs were being delivered with the portables?" she asked.

"Yeah, but I didn't know that!" He shook his head in agitation. "I can't be charged if I didn't know, right? And I'm not saying anything more. You can tell Pope's boss I'll never talk."

"Who is Pope's boss?" She kept her voice level, as if his answer was of no real significance.

"Dunno. The only people I know are Cedro and Pope." He adjusted the sheet, and her heart gave a little kick when he carefully tucked the side over Gunner's back. "So it's best if I keep running."

"The police will stop them," she said. "They just need to figure out who's in charge."

"But if they don't know Pope's boss, how are they going to protect me? Or my mom? They might hurt her if I go back." He made a weak motion to grab his shirt then shivered and settled back against Gunner, as if accepting the need to recharge.

"The police know a lot more about this than I do. They'll keep you safe."

Ricky snorted. "I heard of guys who believed that. It didn't work out well for them."

Nikki had no honest reply. Justin was zealous in protecting his witnesses but he was higher on the hierarchy than Detective Wilson. And if Ricky couldn't provide much information, the police wouldn't be too concerned about his safety. It was actually surprising the drug ring was investing so much effort to find him, considering how little Ricky knew.

But it wasn't her job and though she'd love to help bring down a drug ring, it went against her ethics to grill a vulnerable minor.

"How about a protein bar?" she asked, digging in her pack and holding out a crumpled peanut butter bar.

Ricky grabbed it so fast she pulled out another one, wishing she'd brought more. Hot chocolate would have been helpful too, but he seemed to be warming up nicely. His eye-hand coordination had certainly returned, evidenced by his deft snag of the bar.

She fed Gunner generous handfuls of kibble then poked the burning wood into a more compact pile, opting for a smaller flame. Privately she shared Ricky's worry that they might be followed. At least the hardwood branches she'd gathered threw out maximum heat, along with less smoke than softwood.

On the flip side, the wind was blowing from the west, toward the service road. Hopefully if the fire attracted anyone, it would be a park ranger. And not Cedro's killer.

CHAPTER FORTY-ONE

Ricky seemed to be in a deep sleep, the setting sun spotlighting his face. His color had improved and his breathing was steady, but he remained curled beneath the silver blanket, tucked between Gunner and the fire.

Nikki flipped over their clothes, making sure the heat dried all sides while keeping the fire as small as possible. It would be safer to put it out and hole up in the brush for the night. But Gunner remained pressed against the boy's side, as if sensing that Ricky's core heat was still low.

She tugged on her stiff clothes, grimacing at the sogginess of her hiking boots. But if they remained here, it was important to make sure they weren't being followed. No one would attempt a river crossing, especially in the dark, so that left the mountain trail as the logical approach. If the killer was on that steep slope, he would have been forced to leave his utility vehicle. There'd be no engine sounds to give a warning.

"Stay, Gunner," she said, pulling out her Glock but leaving the pack. She didn't want Ricky to wake up and think he'd been deserted. There was also the unnerving fact that people wanted him dead. He shouldn't be left alone for long.

It was strange they'd chased him so deep into the mountains. He didn't know the leaders so he wouldn't be much help in bringing down the gang, even if he did decide to cooperate with the police. Going after a kid with such ferocity certainly underscored their viciousness.

Cedro hadn't known that Ricky was tagged for a bullet. The gunfire had taken him by surprise. Then he'd been cut down, showing that neither of them was supposed to leave the mountain alive. Andrea had been correct. Cedro truly had been trying to help, leaving him more of an enigma, along with his status in the gang. Nikki picked her way around the alders, the trail as winding as her thoughts. Something nagged at her, a thread she couldn't quite grasp.

She stopped in the sycamores by the clearing, needing to flush her thoughts. To concentrate. Her only job now was to keep Ricky safe, not analyze the workings of a drug gang. The task force had access to informants and usage patterns. And now that Ricky had confirmed portables were part of the distribution scheme, it explained why so many teens had been affected. She'd pass on what she knew, and they'd figure it out.

She scanned the steep slope, confirming that it was reassuringly empty. So was the clearing. She was about to turn and head back when movement caught the corner of her eye.

She froze. Had someone actually followed? She'd hoped the killer had been ordered to return. Or that the game trail was too steep. Or that he'd be too lazy to leave his vehicle. Those hopes might have been a mistake. Maybe so was making the fire.

She strained to see, to distinguish between the rocks and shadows. It could have been an animal—a bighorn sheep or coyote; even a bear would be preferable. But the dusky light made it hard to make out the shape. It hadn't moved again. Or if it had, it was very stealthy.

At least she was between Ricky and any potential threat. With the river at their backs though, they didn't have an easy escape route.

She fingered the gun, her palm clammy. A Glock wouldn't be much protection against a man with an assault rifle, not unless she kept the element of surprise.

Their fire wasn't visible but the smell of burning wood might be noticeable. The breeze blew from the west, building strength over the open expanse between the trees and slope. It wasn't near as gusty as earlier in the day though. If someone was following, hopefully he didn't have a good sense of smell. And she still wasn't sure if the visitor was two-legged.

Then the shadow moved and her worse fear was confirmed. There was no mistaking the man's head. And the outline of a rifle. He moved toward the river, picking his way over the loose shale, pausing every few feet, as if aware there was no place for his quarry to run.

For a moment, her mind and body locked. She had to force her brain to work, to evaluate her options. At the rate he was moving, he'd be at the alders in less than ten minutes. His current path would take him a hundred feet from her hiding spot. Too far away for a decent shot.

Could she shoot him without giving a warning? Likely if she yelled, he'd simply drop and spray her position with bullets. Justin had warned her of these situations, had insisted on simulating this type of decision-making. She'd passed with flying colors. But it had been much easier to shoot when the bullets weren't real.

There was a chance he'd drop his weapon if she called a warning. The fading light favored an assault weapon over accuracy but he wouldn't know she only had a handgun. Whatever her decision, she had to move closer. And that meant leaving her hiding place.

She eased from behind the protective tree and into the alders, so stiff with adrenaline that her legs felt clumsy. Somehow she avoided any cracking twigs, stopping whenever the killer stopped, her throat bone dry.

The setting sun tinged the trees with red and she kept her eyes averted, keeping her vision as sharp as possible. At least that was in her favor, since Cedro's killer was moving directly toward the west. Hopefully he'd be momentarily blinded when she called out a warning.

If she called out. Justin would stress that in this case a warning wasn't feasible and trying to wing someone would be relying too much on luck. Logically she accepted that, but shooting someone in the back left her gut churning with revulsion.

Maybe she wouldn't have to decide. The man was moving slowly, still on the expanse of open ground. Perhaps his lengthy pauses meant he wasn't fully committed to murdering a kid. She hung on to that hope even as she peered through the bushes, waiting for a good sight line.

She could see the man's back now, and his left arm. He was small and wiry, but the assault rifle at his side made up for his lack of stature. Then her breath caught. Because his slow progress wasn't related to a reluctance to kill. Quite the opposite.

He'd been waiting for darkness to begin his killing. Now it was time. And he was pulling on night goggles.

CHAPTER FORTY-TWO

Nikki pulled in a deep breath, steadying her thumping heart. But her hands felt bloodless and the Glock trembled in her grip. She took three more deep breaths, using anger to push away the reluctance.

The man in front of her was a heartless killer. He'd followed in order to shoot a helpless boy and anyone with him, including Gunner. She had to shoot first, and she couldn't wait any longer. Once the sun went down, he'd hold every advantage.

Still, to shoot an unsuspecting person in the back…

When the risk of failure is death, you need to take the highest percentage shot of success. Justin's words tamped down her lingering hesitation and she raised her gun, holding the Glock in both hands, using her dominant eye to aim. Her stance was solid, hands steady. Exhale half a breath. Focus on the target.

She froze, still holding her breath, but now staring through the sights in dismay—because her target had disappeared.

Silently cursing, she dropped to the ground and slipped sideways. The bushes were scant protection but she had to establish the killer's location. And if he'd seen her.

Perhaps he'd simply chosen that moment to move into the alders and it wouldn't take long to pinpoint his position. But her heart was racing, her neck slick with perspiration, as if anticipating a spray of bullets. Worse, she couldn't see him anywhere. She had to move.

She belly crawled toward the game trail, going as fast as she dared, determined to stay between Ricky and the killer. If he hadn't seen her, he'd follow the trail. It was the easiest and quickest way to the river. If he didn't appear on the game trail, that meant he was cutting through the thick brush. And aware of her presence.

She stopped behind a jagged stump and pressed into the mossy ground. The stump was rotting and didn't provide much cover but it would have to do. This part of the trail was free of low hanging branches and offered a fifteen-foot sight line, good enough to make an accurate shot, even in the dying light.

Her stomach churned and her skin felt paper-thin. A rock poked into her hip and mosquitoes crawled over her forehead. But she remained motionless, listening for his approach: the rustle of a leaf, the snap of a twig. The hint of wood smoke was more prominent here and no doubt Gunner could smell the intruder, but he wasn't barking.

She'd told him to stay and guard, and he'd do that. At least until he heard shots. Then he'd likely come running. It was hard for him to follow orders if he believed she was in danger. But if he did come, he'd run right into a bullet.

Unless she was the first to shoot. She had to take the chest shot. No warning, no aiming for extremities.

An owl hooted ten feet above her head. She didn't flinch. Lives were in danger and she remained focused on the open spot of the trail. Her old boss had taught her investigative skills but Justin had strengthened her, mentally and emotionally. She was ready.

So she waited, every sense alert. The smell of pine and the rotting stump surrounded her, but there was no sign of the killer. No cigarette smoke, fly dope or body sweat. Other than the owl and the buzz of mosquitoes, there were no sounds. It felt like she'd been waiting for over ten minutes but she didn't want to check her watch and risk the light giving away her location. He could be close and waiting. Just like her.

And then she heard a crackling as someone pushed through the brush. Faint but unmistakable. Only it wasn't along the trail; it was at least fifty feet away. Her heart sunk. He was avoiding the path, evidently aware of her presence. And in a few minutes it would be completely dark. Ricky would be a sitting duck by the fire.

She scrambled to her feet and sprinted down the game trail, ducking below most of the branches, ignoring the ones that whipped her in the face. She had to beat him to the river. It should be possible. He was forcing his way through the thick brush while she had a clearer path.

But he couldn't be underestimated. He'd followed Ricky this far and also pegged her location when she thought she'd been well hidden.

Her mind swirled over the options—not many—even as she burst into the clearing. Gunner was at her side in an instant, nosing her hand, while Ricky scrambled to his feet, staring with wide eyes.

"Something's wrong isn't it?" he whispered. "Gunner was upset. His growling woke me."

"Yes, we need to move," Nikki said, relieved to see he'd had the presence of mind to get dressed. "We're being followed. He's about ten minutes out, maybe less."

"Where do we go? The river can't be crossed. I couldn't do it in the daylight, let alone at night."

"Follow the river bank. Go about one hundred yards and cut into the brush. Then hide like you've been doing so well for the last week."

"What about you and Gunner?"

"We're going to stay here, meet this asshole."

"I'll wait with you," Ricky said, his voice low but fierce. "This is my fault. My fight."

Nikki grabbed her pack and pulled out some protein bars. He had a warrior's spirit. Had witnessed how ruthlessly Cedro had been cut down, knew this was no game. But she needed to know he was safe.

"The best way to help is by leaving," she said. "He may give up if he thinks you're not here. And he has night goggles so keep that in mind when you're hiding. Now take these protein bars and run."

"I'm going, but just so you know, if you or Gunner are h-hurt, I will talk to the police. Those fuckers can't go around shooting everyone I know."

He slipped away, swallowed by darkness and the sound of the rushing river. Only Gunner's ears revealed his route.

He'd be all right, she told herself. Nothing around the campfire showed he'd even been here. And he was a wizard at hiding. But she had no illusions that the killer would give up. He'd obviously received orders to finish the job. So it was up to her to lead him away from Ricky.

And she needed to hurry. Gunner was growling again, staring in the opposite direction that Ricky had taken. The killer was coming.

"Heel," she whispered, shouldering her pack and jogging along the animal trail, making sure she made some noise. Not too much that he'd be suspicious but enough that he would hear.

The dense brush on the east side of the ridge would be a good spot to make a stand: it had several wooded escape routes. But there was no margin for error. She had to make sure the killer followed. She also needed enough time to cross the flat area at the bottom of the ridge before he emerged from the alders.

Stars twinkled through occasional gaps in the trees but overhanging branches blackened most of the trail. She kept a hand on Gunner's shoulders, letting him guide her along the path. Part of her wanted to stop and listen, make sure the killer had taken the bait. The other part wanted to sprint to safety.

Her heart thumped in her chest, not from exertion but from primal fear. Then she heard Gunner growl and knew the killer had taken the bait. It was time to run.

CHAPTER FORTY-THREE

Nikki raced through the trees, trusting Gunner to keep them on the narrow trail. Even with his guidance, alders whipped her face. She didn't dare slow, knowing her pursuer wasn't hampered by the dark. And judging by the sounds, he was closing the gap.

Gunner seemed to understand the urgency. His pace quickened until he was almost dragging her. But with the increased speed, she stumbled over several roots, barely managing to stay on her feet. They must be close to the open area though. The ground was hardening from soil to rock.

She didn't feel much relief. It would take a long minute to sprint across the clearing. At least, she'd need that much time. Gunner could do it faster. But he wouldn't desert her. He'd run ahead if ordered but once the bullets started, he'd turn on the shooter with a fury. Or try to. He wouldn't make it far before the assault rifle cut him down too.

She tamped down her fear, weighing their options. Keep running and gamble that she could cross the open area before the shooter burst from the alders. Or wait in the brush and try to get off the first shot. An accurate one, despite the dark. It was a toss-up—with lives at stake.

Moonlight filtered through a gap in the leaves, the brush taunting her with its promise of safety. Maybe she should hide. Try to get off a shot. She blinked, her vision distorted by the sudden skylight. It looked as if the killer was crouched at the base of the thick alders. Then the silhouette gestured and she realized it was Ricky, even as Gunner veered toward him.

"This way," Ricky whispered, tugging her off the game trail and down into the brush. He reached around, positioning a branch over the spot where she and Gunner had entered. Then he turned totally still. Only his thin body pressing against her side confirmed his presence.

She tapped Gunner's muzzle, warning him to be quiet. All three of them lay motionless. It was almost pitch black beneath the low-lying branches, with scant view of the trail. There'd be no chance of a shot but with the variance in light, the killer might run past.

Actually, with the man's night goggles and running speed, it was likely he wouldn't notice where she'd ducked off. The rocky ground left no prints, and branches were broken from when she'd passed earlier. She'd told Ricky to hide close to the river but he must have got twisted around. On second thought, it was probably no accident. The kid was unbelievably savvy, and astonishingly brave.

She lay in the prickly brush, one of her hands wrapped around her gun, the other on Gunner's muzzle. A vibration in the ground was the first sign their pursuer was close, followed by the sound of approaching feet. She held her breath, reluctant to even breathe. Then he ran past, and all was silent again.

After a moment Ricky whispered, "Think he'll come back?"

She thought about lying but this kid had already proven his pluck, and his steadiness under fire.

"No doubt," she said. "But he'll have to check the ridge along the canyon first. I figure we have about twenty minutes before he backtracks."

"There's a rabbit path behind us. Can Gunner crawl through low brush?"

"Better than a bunny," she said, picturing the maze of tunnels and tubes he'd conquered at the K9 Center. "But once we get out, I need your promise that we'll split up."

She felt Ricky's grin before he spoke. "Even though I just saved your ass?"

"Even though." She found his hand and gave it a grateful squeeze. "But this guy is locked on finding you. He may not work as hard to chase down me and Gunner. We just have to avoid him until morning."

"What happens in the morning?"

"The police will come."

Ricky gave a disbelieving snort before turning and wiggling deeper into the brush. He held nothing but scorn for law enforcement. At that age, she'd felt the same way. But he was a hot commodity, a link to the drug ring and Pope's murder. Surely the police would come. Even if they didn't, Justin would.

She urged Gunner to follow, deliberately bringing up the rear as they belly crawled in a winding line. In this position, she could turn on her back and get off a shot, in case their pursuer picked up their trail quicker than expected. But he'd have to assume she'd sprinted across the flat rocks and entered the woods on the other side. At least that was her hope.

That optimism was dashed as pinpricks of light flashed through the canopy, accompanied by a vicious flurry of gunfire. The killer hadn't been fooled, not for a minute. He was already on their trail.

"Go!" she whispered, rolling on her back and positioning her gun over her stomach. There wasn't much of a sight line but she had to try. Before he zeroed in on their location and sprayed them with bullets.

Right now, he was skimming the area with a powerful light but his shooting was off target. Actually it sounded as if there was more than one shooter. And the noise was odd. Not just gunfire but a whirring.

Then understanding hit. She jerked up, so quickly the thorny brush grabbed her hair, raking her face and scalp. But that was okay. Everything was wonderful. Because that unique pulsing could only be made by one thing: a helicopter.

CHAPTER FORTY-FOUR

Nikki stood beside Ricky, blankets draped over their shoulders. In front of them, the police helicopter was silent, perched on the flat ground, its powerful lights outlining a sprawled body.

"They had to kill him," Justin said, gesturing at the tactical officers flanking Detective Wilson. "He was shooting at us."

"I'm just glad you came," Nikki said, staring numbly at the knot of people around the body. "Didn't expect help until tomorrow."

"Sonja passed on your message," Justin said. "Then she called back with additional information from her brother. Those details helped convince Wilson of the relevance, and the urgency. Liam mentioned the waterfall but the campfire helped pinpoint your location."

Nikki looked at Justin, understanding passing between them. Liam wouldn't have understood the importance of his meeting with Ricky but he'd redeemed himself by admitting the planned bike deal. It still didn't explain why it warranted a night extraction.

"When you didn't return," Justin went on, "Sonja sensed you needed help. Was very adamant."

Nikki gave a shaky smile, guessing Detective Wilson and the task force hadn't been swayed by any psychic visions. No doubt, Justin had applied pressure, forcing quick action.

Whatever way it had unfolded, Ricky was safe. In the space of ten minutes, they'd gone from running for their lives to being surrounded by law enforcement. It was over. And she was swept by a gauntlet of emotions. Wanted to cheer and laugh and cry, but mostly she wanted to crawl into her bed and sleep.

She sank to the ground, her legs buttery soft. Ricky plopped beside her, still staring at the body of the man who'd hunted him so relentlessly. He reached out, automatically adjusting his blanket so he could wrap his arm around Gunner's neck. For someone who'd never liked dogs, he was certainly drawing much comfort from one.

Justin turned back to the helicopter, and spoke to the paramedic. Minutes later, warm cups were pressed into their hands and the smell of chocolate sweetened the air. Ricky took a big gulp, undeterred by its heat. When he lifted his head, he was grinning at her—a boyish conspiratorial grin—his mouth lined with froth.

She smiled back and took a more cautious sip, relishing the hot chocolate, the feeling of normalcy, and seeing Ricky finally able to relax. He'd have to face a lot of questions later, but for now this was indeed a moment to savor.

CHAPTER FORTY-FIVE

An insistent buzzing jerked Nikki awake. She fumbled for her phone, recognizing she was alone in bed. She had no idea when Justin left, or if he'd even slept. They'd arrived home at three o'clock in the morning, but unlike her, he could operate on scant amounts of rest.

She checked the time. Almost eight o'clock so she'd had five hours of deep sleep. Justin was probably calling with an update. Once the helicopter landed, she'd been separated from Ricky and a detective had taken her report, including how the portables were being used. After that, she'd been shunted aside, only able to imagine Ricky's reunion with his mother. No doubt Justin knew she'd be keen to hear all the happy details.

But it wasn't Justin calling.

"We talked to Ricky in the car," Detective Wilson said, skipping any sort of greeting. "But he refused to give us anything."

"You questioned him last night?" Nikki jumped from groggy to wide awake. "Without his mother present? Or a lawyer?"

"We had a forty-minute car ride," Wilson snapped. "And lives are at stake."

Nikki swallowed her reply. The detective sounded a bit like Justin. Police had many more legal hurdles than a PI, and they could circle the wagons quickly. It never helped to rev them up.

She swung her legs over the bed, her aching muscles reminding her of yesterday's ordeal. It was hard to be civil, feeling the soreness, knowing how drained she'd been last night. And it would have been much worse for Ricky. He'd have been in no shape for a police grilling.

"I need to know if he said anything to you yesterday," Wilson went on. "Especially in that situation, you know, where you were together for so long."

"You mean the situation where he was half-starved and running for his life?" Nikki asked, bristling at the woman's lack of empathy.

"Exactly. He said you and your dog saved his life. It would be natural to confide in his rescuer." Wilson paused as if for effect. When she spoke again, her voice was officious. "As a PI, you have an obligation to tell us. Licenses have been pulled for less."

Nikki jerked to her feet. She didn't appreciate Wilson's tone. Or the threat.

"I told your detective everything I learned last night," she said. "And Ricky doesn't know anything about the ringleader. If he does, he isn't aware of it."

"Well, he's being distinctly unhelpful. Grunting, giving one-word answers, shrugging off my questions. You'd think he'd be grateful. But he's as stone cold as any street banger."

Hardly fair, Nikki thought, tucking the phone between her ear and shoulder, and working the kinks from her arms. As Ricky's mother said, he kept his emotions locked up, and if Detective Wilson expected a teary thank-you she'd be disappointed.

"He's exhausted as well as scared," Nikki said. "Two men he knew are dead. Cedro was murdered in front of him. The only thing he did was take a cleaning job with the wrong people."

"And run off with a packet of cocaine," Wilson said dryly.

"That was impulsive. Pope owed him money. He was only trying to collect."

"Maybe. But we believe he witnessed the murder. Yet he's denying it."

Nikki suppressed a sigh. Ricky was street savvy and following his own belief system. If word got back to the gang that he wasn't talking, he thought they'd leave him alone. She believed him when he claimed he didn't know the leader. He hadn't even been on that path in the woods where Pope's body had been found—Gunner would have picked up his scent.

"So naturally we don't have any recourse but to lay charges." Wilson went on, her voice dripping with fake regret. "I also can't justify keeping a security detail on their apartment."

Nikki spun around, almost dropping the phone. "You must be joking! They followed him into the mountains. Kept chasing, even after the drugs were retrieved. It's obvious the gang leader wants him dead."

"But he's not helping us identify the leader. Meanwhile we have another young OD victim, apparently with matching drug chemistry."

Nikki squeezed her eyes in dismay. "Any ID on the dead shooter yet? I gave pictures of the vehicle plate. And what about the recovered phones? Anything on them?"

"That's classified. But I can tell you we haven't found any gang affiliation. So we need everyone on the street, not wasted on a security detail." Wilson gave a pregnant pause. "Especially since your kid isn't giving us anything."

"How long before the detail comes off?"

"Twelve hours."

Nikki scooped up a pair of jeans and Gunner's collar. This was the only invitation she needed. "I'll drive out now and talk to him."

"Thought you might," Wilson said.

CHAPTER FORTY-SIX

Nikki stopped in front of Ricky's house, noting the Dodge Charger parked thirty feet away. A man and woman sat in the front seats. They didn't challenge her when she and Gunner climbed the steps to the front door.

The door swung open before she even knocked.

"Thank you!" Andrea said, flinging her arms around Nikki's neck. "You brought him home! Ricky told me everything you and your dog did. Come in, come in!"

She closed the door behind them, shutting out the hot sunshine along with the stares of the watchful officers.

"He's still in bed," Andrea said, the dark circles under her eyes prominent. Ricky might be sleeping but it was clear his mother hadn't. "He told me Cedro is dead. Is that true?"

At Nikki's nod, she gave a pained gasp. "It's my fault," Andrea said. "Cedro didn't want to interfere, was afraid to be seen with me. They ordered him to cut off contact. But I begged him to help."

"Who made him so afraid?"

"He wouldn't say." Andrea rubbed her hands up and down her arms. "I didn't even know drugs were involved until you told me. I was furious with him for finding Ricky that job. He felt guilty too. That's why he finally agreed to help, that night in the maintenance shed."

"Could he have been afraid of Pope?" Cedro had driven out to the man's house almost immediately after his liaison with Andrea. Maybe he'd wanted to ask that the gang ease up on Ricky, not realizing Pope was already dead.

"No," Andrea said. "It was someone he called the boss."

"Does the boss work at the track? Is that why he couldn't be seen with you?"

Andrea shook her head. "No, because he picked up pizza once on the way here. Said he was at his boss's house, about forty minutes away. I remember asking if he had another job beside the track and he shut me down."

"What was the name of the pizza place?"

"Don't know. I do remember the pizza had egg on it." Andrea wrinkled her nose. "Cedro said it was his favorite. But Ricky and I didn't like it."

Nikki ran a frustrated hand over Gunner's head. She still had her suspicions about an accomplice at the track. Cedro hadn't wanted to be seen with Andrea, either at the kitchen or around his dorm. His car was still parked there so someone must have driven him from the property...a place that was conveniently loaded with surveillance cameras.

She wheeled toward the door. "I'm going to pop over to the track. Text me a list of Cedro's friends, anyone you can think of. And give me a call when Ricky wakes up."

"Sure, but he'll probably sleep all day. Now that everything is okay, he's dead to the world."

Nikki's hand tightened around the door knob. She didn't want to scare Andrea but the woman needed to understand the situation.

"Then you might have to wake him," she said. "Because whoever wants your son dead is still out there. Nothing has changed simply because he's home."

"But like he told the detective last night, he doesn't know anything. There's no reason to hurt him. Besides, there's a cop car parked outside."

"Which won't be there after eight o'clock tonight. Pope's drugs were contaminated. They're killing people. Police resources are stretched too thin to keep a security detail here."

"Figures." Andrea sank onto the sofa, her shoulders sagging. "People like us never get any help."

Nikki wasn't unsympathetic. She'd gained enough insight from Justin to know that a high-profile family would probably receive more enthusiastic protection. But the rescue last night had cost plenty of taxpayers' money, and Ricky wasn't offering any information. Meanwhile innocent youth were dying.

"I know he's scared," she said. "I was afraid last night too. It's terrifying to be hunted. But someone fears Ricky, or something he knows. It may be a tiny detail. Or maybe it's because he stole a packet of drugs. I don't know. But for everyone's safety, we need his help identifying the leader."

Andrea leaned forward, hands twisting fearfully on her lap, eyes beseeching. "You've always been on our side. So tell me this: Don't you think Ricky would be safer if word got out he's not talking? Because that's what Cedro thought."

Nikki just held the woman's gaze, unspeaking. Considering Cedro's fate, the question didn't require an answer.

Andrea came to the same conclusion. "I'll wake him up," she said "He'll be ready to talk when you come back."

CHAPTER FORTY-SEVEN

Nikki's phone rang just as she was pulling into the Santa Anita parking lot.

"You awake?" Sonja asked. "Justin texted that you were safe and home. And that you found the boy."

"Yes, thanks for calling in the cavalry." Nikki pressed off her ignition. "And also to Liam for giving Ricky's location. I'm at the track now, just following up on a few things."

"Checking on the horses? Or work? Because I wanted to tell you that Liam agreed to enter a rehab facility. He needs more help than I can give. Making a drug deal with a desperate kid was the last straw." Her voice thickened. "And I want to apologize for pushing Gunner to be a drug sniffer. You two should stick to what you do best. You're an amazing team."

Nikki grinned. Gunner much preferred rescuing people, and so did she. Hiding the drug sample around Sugar's stall seemed like weeks ago. But if she hadn't gone to the track to train Gunner, she never would have met Andrea, and been able to help Ricky.

She stared through the windshield at the administration offices, her smile fading. Because Ricky still wasn't safe and the police didn't seem close to a breakthrough. Both Cedro and Pope—and even Cedro's dead assassin—had no known gang affiliations.

Pope had turned out to be an even more minor player than she'd imagined. She had no idea why he'd been murdered but Cedro's death was definitely tied to Ricky. Cedro had abruptly quit his job at the track. Was that because he no longer wanted to work with the gang or because his location at the track was no longer required?

His murder didn't fit. He'd been trusted enough to go into the mountains after Ricky. But once he'd retrieved the drugs and lured Ricky into the open, he'd been shot.

"I'll be coming by the track soon," Sonja said, pulling back Nikki's attention. "Have to pick some horses so I can make up for being off work for so long."

Only a psychic would consider race bets as surefire income. But Sonja already sounded like her old self. Maybe it was good that Liam had bought some contaminated heroin. The overdose had exposed his addiction and now they both accepted the need for professional help. And Sonja's fear about him finding drugs in the wilderness had been justified. She did have a gift.

Nikki palmed her hands over the steering wheel. "Do you feel anything evil at the track?" she asked hopefully. "Any visions that show who wants to kill Ricky?"

"Sorry." Sonja laughed, an airy musical sound that Nikki hadn't heard in a while. "My current views are all through a horse's eyes. I can tell you that Sugar is wondering when that dog lady will come back with some delicious round pink things."

Her voice turned serious. "If you think Ricky is still in danger, I'd be happy to help. I'm driving Liam to rehab this afternoon but tomorrow we could stroll around the backside. Talk to people of interest. Maybe we can even fit in lunch."

"Perfect," Nikki said. "By the way, can you confirm who Ricky asked Liam to call, and give his mountain location?"

"Someone named Cedro. But Liam couldn't sneak my phone until yesterday morning. So that's when he called the guy."

Nikki nodded. It wasn't much help but it explained why Cedro hadn't met Andrea. Once he'd been notified of Ricky's location, he'd taken off. Just not in his own car.

"Please thank Liam for telling Justin the truth," Nikki said. "It saved us."

She ended the call, looking forward to Sonja's insight tomorrow. Even if the psychic angle didn't help, it would be nice to have another opinion. Her picture of Cedro was muddied, and that left her uneasy.

Cedro's ex-wife believed he was low man in his dealings with Pope, while Andrea thought the opposite. One thing for sure, Cedro had been sincere about helping Ricky. And he'd paid for it with his life.

Sighing, she scooped up her backpack and dug around for Gunner's harness. The pack was noticeably lighter than usual. She'd been in too much of a hurry this morning to replenish supplies, and now it was short of protein bars and dog food. She'd also removed the drug sample; she didn't want Gunner and Sugar alerting to her backpack again.

She clipped on Gunner's leash and gave him a loving pat. Finding illicit drugs might not be in their future but he'd saved Ricky's life. And now that Sonja was no longer policing her brother, it was a relief to stop trying to turn Gunner into a sniffer dog.

For now, he could relax while she checked yesterday's security video. And for that she needed Travis Hillman's help.

CHAPTER FORTY-EIGHT

"Mr. Hillman is on the backside now," the security guard said, eyeing Nikki and Gunner from behind the imposing counter. "Is there something I can help you with?"

"Yes, I need to see some video from yesterday morning. Anything you have between six and eleven for the road from the kitchen to the south end parking lot. It's regarding an urgent police matter."

She didn't say she was with the police and fortunately the guard didn't ask for ID. But he also didn't seem inclined to escort her into the video room.

"That's a lot of footage," he said, crossing his arms. "The usual procedure is that you apply online. Once the request is approved, we'll arrange for a technician to gather the file and forward it to an upload address."

That was disappointing. Once he realized she was a PI, the process would turn even slower. It was unfortunate Travis wasn't here. He might have walked her back immediately, especially if he thought it would help Justin. On the other hand, he was on the grounds so maybe it wouldn't take long to find him.

"I'm going to head over to the barns," she said. "Maybe I can find Travis and save you all some work."

"Worth a shot." The guard winked as if aware she was hoping to bypass procedure. "Check out Clockers' Corner. He likes to keep his ear close to the ground."

Nikki gave an appreciative nod then hurried from the office and strode along the mezzanine level of the grandstand. Clockers' Corner was at the top of the stretch, a short walk away. The breakfast nook was a popular spot where owners, trainers, and fans could watch morning workouts while enjoying free coffee and engaging in some friendly banter. And it would save considerable time if she didn't have to search the barns for Travis.

She exited above the bleachers and before the end of the grandstand, keeping Gunner well back. The scenic spot was bustling and an unusual number of wide-eyed children crammed the table area beside the rail. Apparently an intrepid teacher had brought her elementary class for a field trip. The San Gabriel Mountains were always an impressive sight but the children were rightly more interested in the galloping horses.

Travis stood by the rail, talking to a chaperone and beaming like a proud father as horses galloped past.

"Stay, Gunner," Nikki said, motioning with her hand before descending the steps. While a trained dog was less likely to scare a horse than a passel of unbridled kids, a social media photo would give the impression that dogs were welcome by the rail. And no one ever knew what might spook a horse.

Travis nodded at her approach then looked past her, smiling approval when he spotted Gunner well removed from the action.

"Good to see a hero so early in the day," he said, shifting sideways so she could squeeze in beside him. "Hate to see the other guy," he added, staring curiously at the scratches on her face.

"Ran into some rough spots," she said.

"Well, it sounds like quite an accomplishment. You found the kid, and uncovered the use of ghost portables. Well done."

A flush of satisfaction warmed her face, along with surprise. "Were you talking to Detective Wilson?"

"No, Justin gave me a courtesy call. Advised that someone on the task force will be contacting us about an ex-employee, Cedro Rugger. I understand that's the same guy you were asking about?" At her nod Travis gave a heavy sigh. "Heard he's deceased. Apparently they have him pegged as a possible player in a drug ring."

"More than possible. And that's probably why he was working here. To distribute to workers, or spectators."

Travis dragged a hand over his jaw. "Unlikely. We have checks at every entrance, along with cameras. It would be too risky to smuggle in."

"But that's the advantage of the portables. They can get into any venue, with little inspection. Once past security, the drugs are a breeze to distribute."

"Keep your voice down." Travis shifted so that he was between her and the spectators. "Rumors like that are the last thing any track needs. I understand Cedro was associated with a kitchen worker named Andrea Lopez, along with her son, but I'm confident their friendship had nothing to do with drugs. I've done my own check on the woman and she's squeaky clean."

"Yes, but what about Cedro? That's who I'm interested in."

"And that's what the task force and my team will figure out. We're going to examine all the portables. Check out the companies and find out which ones are legit. Thankfully you found the kid and brought him home unharmed. Now you can relax."

She didn't respond to his congratulatory slap on her back. Ricky still needed her help.

"I'd like to see your video from yesterday," she said, firming her voice. "Cedro's car is still parked on the grounds so someone from the track must have picked him up."

"How do you know his car is here? Security just advised me of that."

"Justin must have mentioned it," she said, making a mental note to remove her tracker later today when it wasn't as busy. "So Cedro had to have been picked up on the grounds."

"More likely he walked out one of the backstretch gates."

"No, because my dog lost his scent outside the kitchen. He planned to meet Andrea there but never showed. Someone must have changed his plans. And another thing, he was worried about being seen with Andrea. Was scrupulous about avoiding the cameras."

"If he was trying to avoid our surveillance, you won't find anything in the system. An employee would be aware of the locations."

"But it's impossible to escape them all. Not in a car. You said the track is state-of-the art, with cameras everywhere. Besides, the police are going to be asking for this same info."

Travis shuffled back a step, clearly unwilling to accept that a track employee was involved in a murderous drug ring. But he pulled out his phone and tapped a message.

"I just authorized you to see yesterday's video," he said. "Give my staff the hours, specific location and your upload address. They'll send it along."

She gave a grateful nod. Privately she hoped the technician would let her view it onsite so there'd be a chance of accessing footage from other spots. Best not to mention that though. Travis was already being more than helpful.

She needed to leave now and collect Gunner since she could feel his imploring gaze. However, she lingered when she spotted a familiar horse strolling along the outer rail, only twenty feet away. Both horse and rider looked way more relaxed than the Thoroughbreds in training.

Colleen grinned at Nikki then at the rapt children. Sugar copied her greeting, his neck low and swinging on a loose rein.

"Can we pat him?" a girl in pigtails called.

"Sure." Colleen obligingly stopped Sugar who was instantly swarmed by a score of children along with their hovering chaperone. Sugar stretched his head over the rail, relishing the attention and gently sniffing each little hand.

"He's always hopeful for treats," Colleen said, winking at Travis and Nikki. "He's been fed peppermints here before and has a great memory."

The children were delighted by Sugar's interest, regardless of his motive. Colleen and Sugar were perfect ambassadors. Most of these children had never been close to a horse before. Even the teacher and chaperones became involved, taking pictures and asking questions about the job of a pony horse.

"We're waiting for that black filly to finish her training," Colleen said, pointing at a galloping horse kicking up clods of dirt. "Then we'll escort her back to the barn. Horses are herd animals so they like company. And the calmer and more focused they are, the better they'll race. Sugar is a pro at relaxing others and setting a good example."

According to Sonja, Nikki thought, he was also good at picking horses that could win races. And Gunner certainly liked Sugar. Nikki always respected her dog's judgment.

She glanced over her shoulder. Gunner's ears were pricked but he was following her stay command. It wasn't fair to leave him any longer though, not when his favorite horse was so close. Besides, she wanted to return to the security office and check the video. Tomorrow, she and Sonja planned to visit the backside. Gunner would have plenty of time to see Sugar then.

"I'll bring coffee and breakfast sandwiches tomorrow," Nikki said to Colleen. At the sound of her voice, Sugar's head rose. He swung away from the children and forcefully bumped his nose against Travis's shoulder.

"Sorry." Colleen tightened the reins and corrected her horse. "He's not usually so rude."

Travis chuckled, not a bit annoyed. "He's just a horse. Bumming for treats."

But Nikki was also surprised at Sugar's behavior. It was a good thing he hadn't shoved one of the children with that big head. Maybe she'd fed him too many peppermints while training Gunner. Yesterday he'd certainly given her backpack a rude push.

In fact, Sugar was staring at her, as if anticipating a mint. That didn't explain why he'd expected a treat from Travis though. Sugar hadn't been like that with the children, or any of the other adults by the rail. It had only been Travis he bumped...as if he'd smelled something.

Nikki forced a smile even as fingers of dread chilled her chest. "Do you have mints in your pocket?" she asked. *Please say yes.*

"No," Travis said.

CHAPTER FORTY-NINE

Nikki raced back to the security office, breathless with suspicion. *Travis Hillman involved with the drug ring?* She couldn't believe it. He definitely had access to every nook and cranny of the track, including placement of ghost portables. He could be Cedro's boss. It made sense why Cedro had avoided the cameras if it had been Travis who'd told him to cut contact with Andrea.

But was Travis ruthless enough to order Ricky's murder? That was almost too repugnant to even consider.

Sugar had acted as if he'd smelled drugs on his clothes. Of course, Travis could have been involved in a recent seizure. He might have caught a spectator or worker with drugs. After all, that was part of his job.

She pushed open the office door, feeling like she'd just run a mile.

"You're back," the security guard said, rising to his feet. "Travis confirmed you want video from yesterday. If you give the time and location, we'll gather it up. Have it to you by noon."

"*We* thought it would be easier if I just scroll through it here," she said breezily. "Save some time. Especially since I'm familiar with the system."

"All right, if that's what Travis wants." The guard shrugged and motioned for her to follow. "Keep your dog leashed."

She gave an obedient nod, hiding her elation.

The guard escorted her through a secure door, past several people monitoring a wall of screens, and into a side room. He gave her concise instructions, making sure she was able to toggle between the relevant cameras.

Fifteen minutes later, she was alone in front of the computer. She rolled her chair closer, concentrating on the area around the kitchen, searching for Cedro's distinctive strut. Twice she enlarged the image, thinking she had him. But it wasn't Cedro.

She didn't really expect to see anything. He knew the location of the cameras, had instructed Andrea to meet him behind the kitchen because of its blind spot. The area close to where he'd parked might be more revealing. Because someone had picked him up before he had a chance to enter the kitchen. Likely the same person who'd driven him to the trailhead.

She switched to the coverage of the side entrance, beginning at 6:00 am. At such an early hour, most vehicles were entering, not exiting. Her eyes blurred from staring at the countless vet trucks, horse trailers and feed shipments. A security Jeep rolled by, but it was driven by a female officer. She made a note of the time, 7:07 am, and continued watching, consumed with both hope and dread.

She didn't want to believe Travis was the man calling the shots. He'd given her access to the cameras so likely he had nothing to do with it. However, he'd only authorized her to look at the east entrance. And she planned to check the area around the kitchen, where Gunner had lost the scent, as well as the exits.

However, it was agonizingly slow checking the traffic around the busy kitchen and whoever had picked up Cedro must have stopped in a blind spot, the driver also aware of the cameras. Hillman would definitely know their placement.

She leaned back, squeezing the bridge of her nose. The police would be able to check their video and license plate readers, but that would take time. Meanwhile she had access to all this coverage. Surely there was something.

She'd met Hillman driving toward the main exit yesterday, close to noon. Maybe he'd entered through a backside gate and picked up Cedro. And that meant she was searching too early in the day.

She scrolled back to the exits, fast forwarding over the partial footage of the exterior roads. Hillman had been careful on the track grounds. Maybe not so careful beyond its walls.

It was time consuming, pausing to check every white SUV. Even then, she was only able to see the lane closest to the track fence. She kept peering over her shoulder, afraid the guard would choose this moment to stroll back and check her progress.

But all worries about the guard faded when she caught the rear of a white Bronco merging into traffic, clearly exiting the track. The time on the screen showed 11:47 am. That fit. Andrea said Cedro had texted her, saying he'd pick her up around noon. Someone had changed his plans.

The picture was too grainy to see the license plate or occupants. But if police could establish that Travis had picked up Cedro—a man he claimed not to personally know—it would prove some sort of involvement. Her stomach churned at the idea that Travis could order the killing of a twelve-year-old boy. According to Justin, he'd been a competent detective. Had left the service for higher pay and his love of horses. But criminals hid in all walks of society.

Beside her, Gunner stiffened, giving her enough warning to exit the screen. Seconds later, the security guard strode into the room.

"Finished yet?" he asked, in a tone that suggested her time was up, whether she was finished or not.

"Yes, thanks." Smiling, she rose from the chair. "I was hoping I could also thank Travis but don't imagine he's back yet. He drives a white SUV, right?"

"A Bronco, yes, but only to work. We all use a company Jeep on the property."

"Thank you." And this time her smile was genuine.

She swept from the office, waiting until she was in the privacy of her car before pressing Justin's number.

He answered in seconds. "So you're awake," he said. "I thought you'd need to sleep a bit longer."

"I've been up for a while." She swallowed then forged ahead. "I think Travis Hillman could be involved in this." She followed with a summary of Sugar's reaction and the footage that showed a white Bronco picking up Cedro.

Justin was silent, absorbing the information. It was fortunate he knew horses so well, not scoffing at Sugar's behavior even when it implicated a friend.

"Did Gunner react as well?" he finally asked.

"He wasn't close to Hillman. We were on the grandstand side so I left him at the top of the mezzanine."

"We don't really know if he'd alert to it anyway," Justin said, his tone thoughtful. "How far along are you with his drug detection?"

"Training basically stopped once I started looking for Ricky. But I think he'd pick it up." Her belief strengthened when she remembered how Gunner had lunged toward Hillman's Bronco yesterday, as if picking up a scent.

"Yes, I'm sure he would," she added. "I'll wait here until Hillman returns. See if Gunner reacts the same way as Sugar."

"No! If Hillman's involved, I don't want you near him. If he can go after a kid, he'll have no qualms about murdering anyone. And last night, Nik, it was too close."

Nikki gripped the steering wheel. She knew Justin worried but he'd always supported her decisions. And she did check in with him. That was part of their arrangement, a text system that made sense for an investigator who worked alone.

"Look," he said, slowly, softly. "It's important not to spook him. You found Ricky. Let Wilson's team handle the rest. I'll call her. Suggest she take a close look at Hillman."

"On what basis? She won't give credence to a horse's reaction."

"She should. Equine air scenting has been used successfully by other organizations. And I don't have to give a reason. By the way, they recovered Cedro's body this morning. Thought you'd be the best person to tell Ricky and his mom."

She sighed, feeling her body calm. Despite all the homicides Justin had worked, he never forgot about the pain of the victim's family and friends. And his word was gold; he'd make sure Hillman was thoroughly investigated. Besides, her commitment was to Ricky, not scoping out a drug ring. Still, she couldn't resist one last question. "Did Cedro have a phone on him, maybe some calls from Travis?"

"No phone on Cedro, but two personal phones and two burners were pulled from the shooter. Guy known as Josiah Ortiz, aka Angel. They're with tech now. The phone carriers have already been subpoenaed. And the plate number you gave shows the OHV is owned by the same numbered company as Pope's bungalow."

It sounded like police were close to a breakthrough. And knowing that Justin would keep her in the loop was comforting. Emotion thickened her voice and the words came out husky. "I hope you know how much I appreciate you."

"Your tenacity did this. You won't get many accolades from Wilson but you have mine. In fact, I'll show you tonight." Justin's chuckle was deep and wicked, although he quickly sobered. "Look, Hillman understands police procedure. If he's involved, he'll be worrying about the evidence. Turning desperate. So please, stay away."

"But that would make him a monster. Is he capable of putting tainted drugs on the street? Chasing someone like Ricky?"

"I hope not," Justin said.

CHAPTER FIFTY

Nikki cruised past security's designated lot, sneaking a peek in her rearview mirror. Hillman's white Bronco was nowhere in sight. Probably just as well. She'd be tempted to slip on a tag, find out where and whom he met. But police would be investigating and all evidence had to be legally gathered.

Besides, if Hillman found a tracker, he'd know he was a suspect. No telling what he'd do to cover his trail. This ring had proven to be horrifyingly ruthless.

The track exit was close and she sped through the gates, suddenly eager to leave. Justin didn't make empty warnings. But it didn't mean she couldn't ask Ricky a few questions.

She pulled into the parking lot of a nearby strip mall, scrolled through her pictures then called Andrea.

"Is Ricky awake yet?" she asked, pulling up a recent photo of Travis Hillman. "I need him to look at a picture."

"Yes, he's up. I was just about to call you. We had a talk and he's promised to help."

Seconds later, Ricky spoke on the phone, his greeting surprisingly brief considering what they'd been through. It drove home the fact that he was a reserved kid, and that he'd been well-schooled by Cedro.

"I'm forwarding a picture," she said. "Please tell me if you recognize anyone."

Ricky grunted assent then there was silence except for his breathing and the clacking of dishes in the background.

"I recognize you," he finally said "And Gunner of course. Don't know anyone else."

"Take your time. Expand it."

"I already did. But I don't know any of those other people."

"What about the man third from the left?" She didn't want to lead him but she'd been sure he'd recognize Hillman.

"Nope."

Nikki squeezed her eyes shut. She'd been so certain. Andrea's voice sounded in the background.

"We talked about this, Ricky," she urged. "You need to tell her everything. It's the only way you'll be safe."

"But I don't know him."

"You never saw him before?" Nikki asked. "Maybe with Pope? You said you were at Pope's house when they came."

"Yeah, two men. But I was hiding in a portable on the back of the truck. Never saw their faces, only their legs."

"Did you see their vehicle?"

"Just a glimpse. Brown sedan, maybe a Chevy. Didn't get a good look. Only opened the door a crack. Sorry. Mom told me to help but I can't make up answers."

"Of course not. But maybe you'd recognize a voice?"

"Maybe," Ricky said. "Does that man think I saw him? Is that why the cops are parked outside?"

Andrea's voice came back on the phone. "I'm going to make a late breakfast. Maybe you and Gunner would like to join us? And Ricky can look at more pictures."

"That would be great, thanks." Nikki's stomach rumbled at the prospect of food. Andrea was probably an excellent cook and it would be nice to join Ricky in eating something besides protein bars. It would also be a chance to have him listen to some audio.

Newly optimistic, she wheeled out of the parking lot, only half listening as Andrea recited the best way to make crispy bacon. Ricky hadn't seen Pope's killers, but he might remember a voice. If she couldn't find a recording online, she'd call Hillman and make one. Sounds often jarred memories loose. Naturally Ricky was a little fuzzy. He'd been running for almost a week and had seen the murder of a man he admired.

And now that Andrea had finished reciting the brunch menu, it was time to break the news. "That sounds delicious," Nikki said, blowing out a regretful breath. "I also wanted to let you know that police recovered Cedro's body."

Andrea gave a heavy sigh. "I was worried about that. Especially out there, with all the hungry birds and animals. Thanks for telling me. His ex must be relieved."

"I'm not sure she even knows." Carmen probably wouldn't be too broken up about Cedro's death. The woman had been living in fear, even buying a guard dog whose presence she barely tolerated. "I don't think she's on the police contact list," Nikki added. "They hadn't remained close."

"That's not what I thought," Andrea said. "But I never met the woman. I'm only going off what Cedro said."

Nikki absently rubbed a sore thigh muscle. Cedro's words and actions had always been erratic. But whatever his relationship with his ex, Carmen shouldn't have to learn about it on the news. After having met the woman, Nikki felt a measure of responsibility.

She pulled Carmen's address up on her GPS. It was only twenty miles away. A detour wouldn't take much time. Death notices were usually gut wrenching but this one should be relatively easy.

"I'll join you and Ricky in about an hour," she said, accelerating and moving into a faster outer lane. "See you then."

Traffic was flowing well and she made good time, veering off York Boulevard and into the residential area with few delays. Even the music suited her relaxed mood and there was no need to browse stations.

She was only a block from Carmen's house when her serenity was shattered. A loose dog raced down the middle of the street. A tan pit bull dragging a rope. If it wasn't Ginger, the dog was identical. And she was running a collision course toward Nikki's car.

Nikki jammed on her brakes, swung toward the curb and quickly lowered her window. "Here, Ginger," she called.

The dog responded instantly. She cut to the driver's side and skidded to a stop, her anxious eyes on Nikki. Gunner rose, jammed his nose through the open window and growled a warning.

"It's okay," Nikki said, speaking to both of them as she swung open her door. Something was wrong. Ginger didn't even react to Gunner, just shivered on the pavement, one paw lifted against the car, as if desperate to escape.

Nikki gently ran her hands over the dog's body, wondering if she'd been hit by a car. Ginger's heartbeat was high and she was definitely upset, but she didn't appear physically injured. And she didn't react negatively to Nikki's touch.

Nikki scooped up the thick rope. Carmen's house was only a block away. Probably best to walk. Gunner had his nose out the window and Ginger licked his muzzle, showing her deference. But it would be risky putting the two dogs together in confined quarters.

Controlling Gunner wasn't a concern but the pit bull was an unknown quantity. She was clearly agitated and if she perceived Gunner as a threat, it could get ugly. And it was best to give her a chance to settle before attempting to lead her up the street.

Gradually Ginger's shivering lessened. She still pressed against the car though, periodically lifting her head to the open window, checking on Gunner's presence.

"Let's go home, Ginger." Nikki gave the rope a little tug. The dog didn't move, seeming to draw comfort from Gunner. Nikki sighed, reluctant to get into an argument with a pit bull.

She glanced up the street, hoping Carmen would appear, or even a helpful neighbor. But other than a scatter of parked cars, the area remained deserted.

Maybe a different approach would work.

"Heel, Ginger," she said, and rather surprisingly the dog turned and began walking by her left leg. Ginger gave a last wistful look at Gunner who watched from the car, but otherwise she was the picture of obedience. She really was a nice dog, Nikki thought, reaching down and giving her an approving pat. Ginger lifted her head, accepting the caress, and it was then Nikki caught the flash of red beneath her muzzle.

She knelt on the pavement, searching for the source of the blood. But there was no injury. At least not to Ginger.

Gulping, she continued toward Carmen's house, glancing left and right, apprehensive about spotting a neighbor's injured pet. She was so focused on scanning the surrounding yards, she didn't recognize the vehicle until she was almost beside it.

A white Bronco. And ominously, Carmen's front door gaped open.

CHAPTER FIFTY-ONE

Nikki ran to the front door, her heart racing. Travis Hillman was here. She'd never imagined Cedro's ex-wife might be in danger. But Ginger jerked to a stop, refusing to step inside, slowing Nikki as effectively as a dead weight.

"Carmen!" she called, dropping the rope, wishing she'd grabbed her gun instead of the reluctant dog. "The police are outside. Is everything okay?"

Nothing but silence.

She eased into the spacious living area then stopped and listened. There was no sign of anyone here, or in the kitchen. Nothing was disturbed. Maybe Hillman had slipped out the back door, perhaps falling for her bluff about the police.

Something shuffled behind the kitchen island, accompanied by a woman's trembling voice. "Over h-here."

Nikki stepped closer, peering around the kitchen. Carmen huddled in the corner, arms clasped around her knees. A gun lay at her feet. She barely looked at Nikki, just stared white-faced at the man's body lying by the base of the fridge.

"Is he okay?" Carmen groaned. "I hope he's okay. But he was trying to kill me. I had to shoot."

There was no doubt Travis Hillman was dead. His eyes stared sightlessly and brain matter colored the stainless steel fridge. Nikki quickly averted her eyes.

"Are you hurt?" she asked, reaching for her phone before remembering it was in the car with Gunner.

"Not sure." Carmen gingerly touched her bloody wrist. "The front door hit me when that strange man burst in. He was waving his gun, asking crazy questions about Cedro and where he kept his drugs. Damn dog didn't do anything."

"I'll call for help." Nikki glanced around the counter. "Where's your phone?"

Carmen just groaned, rocking back and forth, all the while staring disbelievingly at the body.

Nikki hurried around the kitchen island, shoved aside a warm pizza box and checked the counter. A charger was plugged in the wall but no phone was visible.

She was still scanning the counter when realization hit: The pizza box was warm. Keeping her back to Carmen, she raised the cover. The untouched pizza was loaded with sausage, bacon and cheese. A yellow-yoked egg crowned the center. An egg...

Movement rustled. She turned, smoothing her expression. But understanding came too late. Carmen still sat on the floor but now the gun was in her hand. And it was pointed at Nikki.

"You shouldn't have come here," the woman said, her voice calm. No sign of shock now. "And you shouldn't have helped that bitch find her thieving kid. Cedro was mine until that slut came along."

"Cedro?" Nikki willed her whirling brain to steady. "You weren't afraid of him?"

"Of course not."

Nikki gaped, realizing now why Cedro had seemed like such an enigma. Carmen had painted a picture of a wife beater. And Nikki had let the woman shape her opinion, believing Andrea to be the biased one.

"I loved him," Carmen went on. "Shouldn't have sent him to the track. Then he never would have met her."

"You sent him?" Nikki repeated, feeling like she was floundering in thick mud.

"You still don't get it, do you?" Carmen sneered. "Cedro did everything I said. They all did. It was a great gig. In and out, no fear of starting a turf war. But Pope's habit hit hard. He was cutting it with fentanyl, stretching the supply. I had to take him out. Couldn't have the cops looking closer at those dead kids." Her lip curled in disgust. "And then you had Hillman coming here, running scared. Afraid you were getting too close."

Nikki stared with growing horror. Carmen had no regrets for the deadly contamination. Her only concern was about getting caught. And Hillman had been her right-hand man.

"The police are outside," she said, trying to keep her voice calm. "Put down the gun, and we'll go out together and explain. Sounds like you had to shoot Hillman in self-defense."

Carmen gave a disbelieving snort. "There's no police outside. And I shot Hillman with my own gun. That's hard to explain. But he was nervous. Wanted to quit the whole operation. And I can't pin this one on Angel."

"What was Angel's role?" Nikki's gaze skipped to a magnetic knife block, the shiny blades almost within reach. It was human nature to brag, so if she could just keep Carmen talking…

"Angel did my wet work. He enjoyed killing. But he's dead now, because of you." The smugness slid from Carmen's face. "They're all dead now except for that juvie thief."

"Ricky didn't plan to steal." Nikki deliberately said his name, hoping to goad Carmen into talking more. "He was only trying to collect his pay. And he doesn't know anything about you."

"That's what he thinks. But that junkie Pope brought him to a meet. I couldn't risk it. Wanted him taken out earlier but Cedro resisted. Promised me the kid could keep his mouth shut."

Carmen gave a bitter laugh, the lines deepening around her mouth. "Cedro claimed he never wanted children. Then he met that boy. It was sickening how he talked about him. *He* was the reason Cedro left me, just as much as the kid's slut mother."

Nikki faked a sympathetic nod, her horror growing. Carmen's hatred for Ricky and his mother was palpable. The woman was a vindictive killer as well as a superb actress. She'd made Pope sound like the brains, and Cedro a hot-tempered ex who she'd kicked to the curb.

"So you sent Angel into the mountains," Nikki said, keeping eye contact with Carmen even as her hand inched toward the knives. "You told him to kill Cedro as well as Ricky. What did Hillman think of that?"

"He knew it had to be done. He'd warned Cedro to stop seeing that woman. And he went with Angel to take care of Pope."

Carmen's voice turned almost wistful. "Too bad it wasn't Ricky dipping into that bad coke. Cedro might still be alive. But I'm through with the chatting. And you can forget about going for a knife."

She rose to her feet. Raised the gun.

"Wait!"

But Carmen's mouth flattened and it was clear there'd be no more talking.

Nikki dove behind the island, knowing her only chance was to race down the hall and onto the street. At least the front door was open.

The gunshot sounded loud. The top of her head burned and bits of ceramic exploded in the air. But her arms and legs still worked. She scrabbled past Hillman's body, driven by primal fear, waiting for a bullet to rip into her back.

But there was no second shot. Only Carmen's curse and a screech of pain.

Nikki was half crawling, half running. Almost out of the kitchen. At first the sounds didn't register. She didn't want to slow, to look back. But now Carmen was hollering commands, her voice mingling with a dog's growls.

Nikki peeked over her shoulder. Ginger's mouth was locked around Carmen's wrist, the gun lying benignly on the floor.

"Stop!" Carmen screamed. "You dumb dog. Stop! Down! Quit!"

One of the commands must have meant something, even if Carmen didn't know which one to use. Ginger's body language changed. She released Carmen's wrist, backed up and dropped to the floor, her tail tucked in submission.

Nikki spun around. Her eyes met Carmen's hate-filled ones and they both charged for the gun. But Nikki was on the floor and further away. She knew it was too late even as a tawny shape launched over the kitchen island, straight as an avenging angel.

Carmen raised her arm, just in time to protect her throat from Gunner's gaping jaws.

Nikki rushed over and scooped up the gun. Only then did she speak. "Quit, Gunner."

It took a repeat of the command for him to release his hold and step back. But he kept growling, his furious eyes on Carmen, daring her to move.

"Good dog," Nikki said, warily checking on Ginger. She didn't want to shoot but Ginger might decide to attack again, now that Nikki was the one holding the gun. And Carmen was looking a little too hopeful, her eyes swiveling between the two dogs, as if calculating the best way to provoke a fight.

"Out, Ginger." Nikki pointed toward the door. It might have been the word or the gesture, but the dog rose and trotted outside, as if relieved to have some clear direction.

Nikki followed, quickly tying her to the outside step. Then she shut the door and hurried back to Gunner's side.

"Dumb fucking dog," Carmen muttered. Her hand was pressed over her torn forearm, the same side as her bloodied wrist. Obviously Ginger had grabbed her gun hand earlier, likely when Carmen had shot Hillman. The dog was simply doing what she'd been trained to do, stopping the aggressor.

Carmen looked up at Nikki, her eyes black pits of venom. "You wrecked everything. And why! You did all this for a loser kid?"

Nikki sagged against the counter, drained of everything except relief. It was over. Ricky was safe. He'd be able to return to his normal life. School, biking with his friends, and a future. Likely it would involve something outdoors.

Carmen continued to spew profanities about her stupid dog and a loser kid named Ricky. Gunner didn't like her attitude. He half-rose and thankfully the woman quit talking.

Nikki straightened, her gaze sweeping to the window where she had a clear view of Ginger's beautiful head.

"You're wrong about Ricky," she said. "And you're very wrong about your dog."

CHAPTER FIFTY-TWO

Nikki relaxed on Sonja's verandah, watching the two dogs race around the paddocks. Ginger had greeted Gunner like an old friend, licking his face then enticing him into a boisterous game of tag.

"She's doing so well here," Sonja said, beaming a proud smile. "Gentle with all the animals. Doesn't have a relationship with them like a herding dog, but certainly respectful. And look how good she is with Gunner."

"It's nice you're giving her a home while we figure out what makes her tick."

"Actually, I want to provide a permanent home."

Nikki grinned, raising her arms in triumph. She'd hoped the dog would win over Sonja but hadn't expected it to happen so fast. It had only been three weeks since Carmen's arrest, and Justin was still working on having her relinquish Ginger's ownership. Nikki had no doubt it would happen. Justin could be ruthlessly persuasive. And it was wonderful that Sonja was opening her heart again. No doubt, her paddocks would soon be filled with other needy rescues.

"I thought you never wanted a dog?" Nikki asked, still grinning. "That this place was only for chickens and hoofed animals?"

"I want this girl. She's special."

"We need to figure out if she has any triggers besides guns," Nikki said. "Although I'm very grateful she reacts to them."

Ginger hadn't been able to protect Hillman from a bullet but the dog had certainly saved Nikki. And given Gunner enough time to finish the job.

"I'm glad you told me to leave the window open," Nikki said, "that first time I drove to Carmen's house. Did you know Gunner would need to jump out?"

"Just a feeling. I couldn't completely shut everything down."

"And I'm grateful for that." Nikki rubbed her arms. Thinking of Carmen's ruthlessness still left her chilled. The woman had met Travis Hillman years ago when she'd been dealing drugs and he'd been the arresting officer with the LAPD. That encounter had led to a sexual relationship and eventually into drug trafficking. Despite their history, Carmen had killed him without hesitation. And she'd had Cedro killed as well.

"Want to move to the sunny side of the verandah?" Sonja asked.

"I'm good. The coffee and critters will warm me," Nikki said, reaching for her mug and giving her friend an appreciative smile. She didn't want to dwell on the evil in the world. Wanted to be able to leave work behind and enjoy all the good things in life, to learn to compartmentalize as well as Justin. It would take awhile but she was learning.

"When did they leave the track?" Sonja peered down the driveway, almost bouncing with excitement. "You're sure Justin's bringing Ricky?"

Nikki nodded, heartened by the way Ricky and Andrea were responding to Justin. If anyone could improve their opinion of law enforcement, it would be him. He knew when a little boost could make a big difference in someone's life.

Gunner was the first to hear the familiar rumble of Justin's truck. He raced to the front of the house, tail wagging. Ginger followed, not sure why he'd stopped playing but happy to follow his lead. Nikki had planned to leash Ginger when the visitors arrived but wondered now if it was necessary. So far, it seemed the only thing that concerned the dog was when someone pulled a gun.

In fairness to Ginger though, it was wise to be cautious. And Sonja needed to anticipate potential problems. Nikki rose from the chair, glancing around for the leash, but Sonja had already scooped it up.

"Come, Ginger," Sonja called, looking proud when the dog raced up the steps and sat by her feet. "That Carmen woman must have been an idiot. Not counting Gunner, this is the sweetest and best-trained dog I've ever met."

Nikki nodded, impressed that Ginger was already looking to Sonja for leadership and not showing any hostility toward the truck.

Ricky was the first to open his door and scramble out. He dropped to one knee and gave Gunner an enthusiastic hug then quickly dropped his arms, embarrassed when he saw he had an audience. But when Justin stepped out and copied his greeting, Ricky crouched back down again, almost knocking Gunner sideways with the force of his pats.

"Justin's so cool," Sonja whispered. "That kid is already looking up to him."

The greeting with Gunner also shaped Ginger's behavior, reinforcing that the visitors were friendly. She watched from the verandah, displaying nothing but curiosity.

"Let's take her closer and see how she does," Nikki said, boosted by the fact that she'd been so friendly when Nikki had first visited Carmen's house.

By the time they descended the steps, Andrea had climbed down from the passenger side and rounded the truck. She smiled in greeting but remained by the bumper, obviously warned by Justin not to crowd Ginger.

"Is that the dog that bit Cedro's ex?" Andrea's smile widened. "I like her already. Ricky and I made her some dog treats. And we have a whole other batch for Gunner. Hope they like them."

"They're peanut butter," Ricky said, rising to his feet. "They have to like them. By the way, Mom said this belongs to you."

He reached into his back pocket and tossed Nikki the tracker. "Wish I had come back and grabbed that jar. You and Gunner would have found me quicker. And Cedro might still be alive."

His face brightened when he spotted Ginger. "So that's Cedro's dog. He taught her lots of tricks. Made me watch them on his phone."

Nikki started to caution him to go slow but Ricky had already rushed up and stuck out his palm. "High five, Ginger."

Ginger sat and pressed her right paw against his open hand. "See," Ricky said. Then he made a face and plugged his nose. "Yuck, something stinks around here. Smell it, Ginger?"

Ginger rolled over on her back, swiping at her curled lip with both paws, looking as disgusted as Ricky.

"And this is the best trick." Ricky unclipped her leash and pointed toward the verandah. "Get me a beer, Ginger."

The dog turned and raced up the steps, deftly poked the screen door open and disappeared inside. No one spoke. Everyone but Ricky watched in stunned silence.

Moments later, Ginger triumphantly emerged from the house with a silver can in her mouth.

She trotted straight to Ricky and placed the can in his waiting hand. He accepted it as though a dog delivered him beer every day.

"Can I drink it, Mom?" he asked, turning to his mother.

"It is non-alcoholic," Sonja said, sputtering over her laughter. "I had them here for Liam. But how did she open the fridge?"

Ricky shrugged and snapped open the cap, clearly not considering it a big deal. He tilted his head and took a long swallow while Ginger waited, eager for his next command.

Lowering the can, he swiped his mouth with the back of his arm. "She does all kinds of stuff like that," he said. "Cedro really missed her but couldn't have her at the track. He was always showing me videos. Right from when he got her as a pup."

Justin was chuckling but Nikki knew he'd take a deep look at Cedro's video and figure out the range of commands. No wonder Carmen was fixated on killing Ricky. Not only had he seen her with Pope but he'd likely seen her face in some of the dog clips. It also explained why Angel had taken the time to collect Cedro's phone after he'd shot him.

Nikki felt a reluctant admiration. Cedro had been a heck of a dog trainer. Even from the grave, that man continued to surprise.

"Is this where Liam lives?" Ricky asked, glancing around as if expecting to see him.

"Yes," Sonja said. "But he's in rehab now. He wanted to apologize though. Knows he shouldn't have asked you to make that trade. And he wants to give you something."

She hurried around the side of the house and reappeared pushing a black mountain bike. Then leaned it against the verandah and stepped back, her smile as wide as her inviting arm gesture.

Ricky's eyes widened. "But I can't do the deal anymore. And I don't have enough money saved, not for a bike like that."

"He wants you to have it," Sonja said. "As a gift. And an apology."

"Can I have it, Mom?" Ricky looked from the bike to his mother, his voice pleading.

"Maybe," Andrea said. "We'll have to talk about not cutting classes." But it was obvious from her big smile that the bike would be going home on the back of Justin's truck.

"I'll never skip again. Promise!" Ricky rammed his fist in the air and charged forward, reverently sliding his hands over the handlebars. "Sweet," he muttered, totally engrossed with the gear shift.

He raised his leg over the seat then paused, his gaze locking on Nikki. He leaned the bike against the verandah and hurried over, surprising her with a fervent hug.

When he stepped back, his eyes glistened. But he made no effort to wipe away the tears, and when he spoke his voice was unapologetically thick.

"Thank you," he said.

OTHER BOOKS BY BEV PETTERSEN

Jockeys and Jewels
Color My Horse
Fillies and Females
Thoroughbreds and Trailer Trash
Studs and Stilettos
Riding For Redemption
A Scandalous Husband
Backstretch Baby
Shadows of the Mountain
Along Came A Cowboy
Grave Instinct (Nikki Drake K9 Mystery)
Repent (Nikki Drake K9 Mystery)
Bone Trail (Nikki Drake K9 Mystery)
A Pony For Christmas (Novella)

About The Author

USA *Today Bestselling Author* Bev Pettersen is a three-time nominee in the National Readers Choice Award as well as the winner of other international awards including the Reader Views Reviewer's Choice Award, Aspen Gold Reader's Choice Award, Write Touch Readers' Award, Kirkus Recommended Read, and a HOLT Medallion Award of Merit. She competed on the Alberta Thoroughbred race circuit and is an Equestrian Canada certified coach.

Bev lives in Nova Scotia with her family—humans and four-legged—and when she's not writing novels, she's riding. If you'd like to know when her next book will be available, please visit her at www.BevPettersen.com